ON THE PRECIPICE

The rear corner of the wagon dangled over the cliff. The wagon seemed precariously balanced. Blake heard Penny moan, then he grimaced when he saw her head slowly rise from the driver's box. The whole wagon seemed to quiver.

"Don't move, Penny."

She seemed confused. She looked at Blake, then at the wagon. Her eyes widened with fear.

"We've got a problem," Blake said.

"Damn right we do," answered Moses. "I can't fly."

Blake worked his hand from beneath the harness and slid off his mule, stepping over the contorted neck of the mule he had shot.

"What happened?" Penny asked, unable to disguise the fear in her voice.

Blake eased to the end of the wagon, glancing warily up the grade at the three Donner men who seemed torn between charging the wagon or holding back for fear it might fall over the edge. Blake didn't understand. This was the perfect opportunity for them to attack.

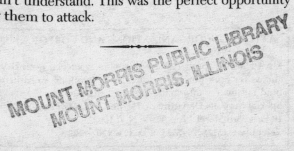

Books by Will Camp

Choctaw Trail
Vigilante Justice
Blood Saga
Escape from Silverton

Available from HarperPaperbacks

ESCAPE FROM SILVERTON

WILL CAMP

HarperPaperbacks
A Division of HarperCollins*Publishers*

This is a work of fiction. The characters, incidents, and dialogues are products of the author's imagination and are not to be construed as real. Any resemblance to actual events or persons, living or dead, is entirely coincidental.

HarperPaperbacks   *A Division of* HarperCollins*Publishers*
10 East 53rd Street, New York, N.Y. 10022

Cover illustration by Tony Gabriele

First printing: May 1995

Printed in the United States of America

HarperPaperbacks and colophon are trademarks of HarperCollins*Publishers*

❖ 10 9 8 7 6 5 4 3 2 1

For David McHam,
who taught me much about writing
and editing

The gray clouds, their bellies swollen with snow, seemed to snag on the jagged peaks of the San Juan Mountains. The cold breath of winter howled over the mountains and along the cliff road which paralleled the noisy waters of the Animas River. The freight wagon, creaking and groaning as it climbed the road to Silverton, would be the last to make it into town before the season's first major snow and perhaps the last to reach Silverton for the winter.

The driver, bundled in a heavy coat and wearing thick gloves, studied the road in the dwindling daylight.

"Four miles, Pug, and we'll be there," he said to his companion, a narrow-faced man with a shotgun resting on his knees.

The guard glanced over his shoulder to see if they were being followed. He shivered. "I'm ready to thaw out and find me one of them fancy ladies who can get my blood to boiling."

"You ain't got the money for a fancy lady, Pug. All you can afford is an old scrawny one with bad teeth and crossed eyes."

Pug shrugged. "I know where I can get all the money I need."

He twisted in his seat and bounced his fist off the tarp snugged over the wagon sideboards. Hidden beneath the canvas were four strongboxes filled with payrolls for the Montezuma, Happy Jack, Belcher and Buckeye mines.

Barney, the driver, nodded. "We could split the hundred thousand dollars, but there'd be a lot of angry miners in Silverton."

Pug laughed. "But a lot of fancy ladies all happy and satisfied."

The driver drew his coat sleeve across his chapped and cracked lips. "You think anybody'll figure out we're hauling the payrolls?"

"As much as we freight between Silverton and Durango, fellows'll think we're bringing in another load of winter supplies. I'll be glad when the damn railroad line's finished into Silverton."

"You idiot," Barney shot back, "the railroad'll put us out of business. The freight company won't need as many wagons and men."

Pug nodded. "I figure on joining the railroad, being one of them conductors who keeps the fire going in the passenger cars. Yes, sir, I won't be freezing my bones any more."

The clouds sagged over the mountains and began to spit snow at the solitary freight wagon.

Barney tugged his hat down tighter. Pug, who had resisted wearing gloves so he could handle the shotgun if necessary, kneaded his stiff hands together.

Rattling the reins, Barney whistled at the six mules pulling the wagon and their drooping ears flicked up for an instant as the wagon crawled up another rise. The mules strained against their harnesses and their iron-shod hooves clanked against the hardrock roadbed as a blast of cold air swooped over the mountain, carrying snow.

Pug balanced the shotgun across his legs as he clapped his hands, trying to generate some warmth. He had been jumpy much of the way from Durango, but with Silverton—and a warm stove—just a few miles away, he relaxed. The freight company had tried to keep this payroll run secret, hoping to disguise it as little more than a final load of supplies before winter set in. This was the last payroll run until spring and everyone—miners and road agents—knew it was coming, though not necessarily how and when.

Despite the wagon's slight load, the mules fought the cold, the incline and the thin air that made breathing difficult in the high mountains. The animals trudged up the rise in the road, then faltered, the lead mules tossing their heads and hesitating.

"Whoa, boys, what is it?" Barney called.

"Probably a rock slide," Pug said, grabbing his shotgun and standing up to inspect the road. He stared into the veil of falling snow, trying to make out what had spooked the mules.

For a moment, he saw nothing, then three forms with guns drawn suddenly appeared through the curtain of falling snow. "Gunmen," Pug said to Barney. "What do you want?" Pug yelled at the men.

"The payrolls," one snarled.

Pug slowly eased his shotgun around toward the men, then tried to bluff them. "Payroll? What the hell you think we are? This is just another load of groceries before the snows set in."

The three men laughed.

Pug squinted at the gunmen, their faces were covered with masks up to their eyes. One of the robbers grabbed the harness of the lead team and stood with his gun pointed at Pug. The other two robbers advanced on opposite sides of the team.

"Drop the shotgun," one of them yelled.

Pug hesitated, then looked at Barney.

The driver nodded. Pug tossed the shotgun to the ground and it clattered on rock, then tumbled over the ledge toward the river.

"Fool," said the gunman nearest Pug. He pointed his pistol at Pug's chest, then fired.

The wind muffled the gunshot as Pug fell dead in the seat.

"Why'd you do that?" Barney screamed. "He dropped his gun like you said."

The robber beside Barney laughed. "We planned to kill you all along."

Tossing the reins aside, Barney bolted up and jumped over the seat, scrambling across the canvas cover. "Don't shoot," Barney shrieked.

As he stumbled, the robber shot him twice in the back. Barney collapsed on the canvas, convulsing for a moment, his arm sliding over the sideboard, then freezing in death.

The robber, his gun still smoking, laughed. "Let's get the money to town, boys, before somebody finds the wagon and bodies."

The wind whistled over the silver-ribbed San Juan Mountains, its icy breath invigorated by the six inches of fresh snow blanketing Silverton. It was November in Colorado and the first major snow had fallen overnight. The air was frigid in Silverton, too damn cold for anything to sour except Blake Corley's luck. His luck had been bad for months. At least winter would end come spring, but Blake didn't know if he could last that long the way his luck had been going.

Hefting the pick over his shoulder, he struck the jagged quartz edges of the tunnel he had scratched out of Anvil Mountain. All he had to show for his hard work was callused hands, ragged clothes and a disposition as rough as the stone wall resisting his pick. He had arrived in the summer, figuring his luck was better than that of those who had been around longer. Blake bought out a promising claim he now realized had been salted by its previous owner, Patrick Haney. Haney was as unscrupulous as a room full of politicians, Blake had decided, but he reached that conclusion too late to find Haney or to demand his five hundred dollars back.

Blake had heard of men going crazy during winters in these mountains. As the snow piled up outside, he knew he should never have sold his Kansas farm and left for the silver fields. He would still have been in Kansas had Tricia Underwood accepted his marriage proposal. She hadn't and he gave up farming for mining, a lamentable choice. At least when he had farmed, he had been able to grow food to sustain himself, but he couldn't eat rock and he couldn't spend the variety he kept digging out of his worthless claim.

Even if he struck silver or gold, he wondered if it was worth the risk. Mining was dangerous work to begin with and there was always the chance of getting shot if your claim showed promise. Men killed for money in these parts. Just the day before two freighters had been murdered not three miles from Silverton. Rumor said the two dead men had been carrying the payrolls for four mines.

The candles at the end of his diggings cast a quivering light upon the walls. Gusts of wind would shove their way deep in the tunnel and set the flames to dancing. The candles flickered like Blake's hope for riches. Blake attacked the quartz wall with his pick, cursing his luck and the approaching winter. Then all at once, he took his pick and tossed it aside. If he worked this worthless hole in the ground much longer, he would likely go crazy. If he stayed the winter in Silverton, he would go crazy for sure. He picked up a candle, leaving the others to burn themselves out, then marched toward the mouth of the tunnel.

Blake bent his five foot ten inch frame as he marched down the narrow rock passage. He was a hundred and sixty pounds of muscle and gristle and his skin was pale from working in the mine's darkness. His hair and eyes were the brown of the worthless rock he had carried from his mine. As he neared the mine entrance, he blew out the candle and tossed it aside, picked up his heavy coat and slouch hat, then put them on before emerging into the brisk air of a dying day. He stood for a moment staring at the yellow lights of Silverton and the foolish men like himself scurrying to find relief from another day's misery.

He trudged through the snow to the one-room shack that came with the claim and shoved the door open. Small, poorly constructed, hard to keep warm and barely big enough for a man to turn around in, the shack was Blake's home. His sod-house in Kansas had been better. He used matches on the table to light his single lamp, its globe broken. The lamp cast jaundiced light across the room as he shoved wood into the small corner stove and began to build a fire for heat and supper once he returned from town. The wood began to pop and crackle as the flame took hold and gradually the room began to warm.

A sudden gust of wind shook the cabin and Blake shuddered. He knew he must escape Silverton but that meant traversing forty miles of snow and cold along a treacherous mountain road that clung to the sides of rugged mountains. Dangerous as that was, he knew it would only take a matter of days. Spending a winter in Silverton would take months.

Though he was hungry, nothing gnawed at him more than his desire to flee Silverton. He figured he could manage enough money to buy passage on the next outbound stage, but stages ran infrequently, if at all, once the snows set in. He may have waited too long and though it was late, he couldn't wait until morning to find out about the next stage. Stepping to his bed, he pulled his holster and pistol from beneath the straw mattress. He strapped the gun belt around his waist, then yanked his hat down and buttoned the top of his coat. Without killing the lamp or checking the stove, he marched outside into the wind and headed toward town, a quarter of a mile away. He cursed the endless carpet of snow that gave the earth a soft, eerie glow.

At the edge of town, he turned toward the Animas Freight and Stage Station, crossing Blair Street where a dozen brothels catered to the carnal needs of the miners. Blake's cold cheeks flushed at the sight of a half naked prostitute waving at him from her second floor window. He pulled his coat tighter and marched down the middle of the virtually abandoned street.

He turned down a side street toward the stage station. The buildings, all with high pitched roofs, were caked with the wet snow. Smoke trailed out of stovepipes, leaving the air thick with the aroma of burning pine. At the freight company office, Blake stepped on the plank walk and stomped his boots against the wood, kicking off clumps of the wet snow. He coughed into his hands, then rubbed them together before grabbing the cold doorknob and entering the warm office.

Three men sat around a pot-bellied stove, leaning back in their chairs and extending their socked feet toward the warmth. A vapor arose from the men's wet boots as they dried in front of the stove. The three men stared sullenly at him. One man wore a patch over his left eye. Another ran his fingers through a bushy red beard that converged at his ears with a disheveled red mop. The third scratched a nose as crooked as the road to Durango.

"Who runs this place?" Blake asked, taking off his hat.

"I do," said a surly voice at the back of the office. "Alfred Donner's the name. Who be you?"

Blake looked from the stove to the rear counter. A burly man with leathery skin, whisker-stubbled cheeks and eyes as black as his disposition stared back.

"Blake Corley's my name."

The three men at the stove snickered. "He's the one that bought the Haney claim," said the red head. The other two men laughed.

Ignoring them, Blake nodded at Donner. "When's the next stage out of Silverton?"

"Next spring, Blake." Donner crossed his arms over his chest as if he enjoyed Blake's disappointment.

"I need to get to Durango," Blake said.

"The hell you do," Donner replied, shaking his head.

Blake nodded. "Isn't there something you can do about it.

Donner spat on the sawdust floor. "Now that's a damn

shame, but I got other problems, like yesterday's robbery. You hear about that, Corley? Payrolls to four mines were stolen and two company men were shot dead." Donner pointed to two coffins in the back corner. "They need to get to Durango, too, but they don't seem to be in as big a hurry as you."

The three men around the stove laughed again.

Blake stared at them

Donner shook his head. "You waited too long. The company doesn't take passengers on the road and very little freight after the first snowfall."

"You know where I can buy a horse or a mule?"

Licking his lips, Donner studied Blake, then spat toward the coffins. "Blake, you're a day late and a dollar short on everything. Guess we should expect that from someone foolish enough to buy the Haney claim. Where you from? You're bound to be a flatlander."

"Kansas."

The station operator nodded. "I figured as much. When winter comes, most folks send their livestock down to lower country where there's more grazing. People that keep a horse or a mule aren't of a mind to sell it by the time of the first snow. Like I said, you're a day late and a dollar short. I suppose next you'll want some fresh vegetables or some spring flowers."

Blake turned and started for the door.

"Another piece of advice, Blake. Don't go stealing no horse either or the sheriff'll be on your tail. We got him trying to figure out who robbed the company and he's gonna be suspicious of anybody who leaves town. You wouldn't want to get shot, him thinking you was a robber now would you?"

Blake let out a slow breath and moved for the door.

"Damnation," Donner said. "I just had an idea that might get you to Durango, Corley, if you know how to drive a freight wagon and a team of mules."

Blake turned around. "I've driven farm wagons and mule teams."

"Six mules or two?"

"Two."

Donner stroked his whiskered chin. "Come back tomorrow around noon and I'll see what I can do for you."

"I'm obliged."

Blake replaced his hat as he marched out the door and into the breeze. He retraced his route, but as he crossed Blair Street he heard shouts and saw a half dozen men pointing toward Anvil Mountain.

Glancing toward the mountain, he caught his breath. Something was burning.

"Ain't that the old Haney claim," somebody called.

Blake gritted his teeth, then raced toward his shack. "Dammit," he cried, wondering with every step what else could go wrong.

When he finally reached the site of his cabin, there was nothing he could do except absorb the heat. There being nothing anyone could do, no one came to fight the fire. Blake suffered his loss silently, the crackle of the flames and the howl of the wind the only response to his thoughts. Then, after the flames turned to embers and the embers sizzled beneath in the snow, he retreated to his tunnel and slept on the hard rock floor.

3

Penny Heath felt the tears welling in her eyes, then streaming down her rouged cheeks as she stood in her gown before the hard gaze of Belle Farthing.

"You're pregnant, aren't you?" Farthing walked around Penny, studying her as emotionlessly as a rancher assesses cattle. Farthing was as hard as the granite in the surrounding mountains and almost as big. Some said she was quite the looker in her younger days, but that was more than a dozen years and a hundred and fifty pounds ago. Her red hair was immaculately combed, but everything else about her had been distorted by years in the trade. Her eyes were dull, her jaws jowly, her arms flabby, and her figure drooping. She tried to hide her lost beauty behind the rings she wore on her fingers, the beads on her necks, the diamonds on her ears, and even the anklets on her legs. She wore so much jewelry that as she wobbled through the brothel she rattled like a wagon in motion. "This ain't your time of the month, Penny. You're pregnant."

Turning to avoid Belle's gaze, Penny sighed. She knew she was beginning to show, but she had hoped no one would notice until she could figure out what to do. She was a fool, though, to think Belle might overlook her condition indefinitely.

"Answer me, girl," Belle cried out. "There's men in the parlor that have been asking about our fair-haired beauty."

Penny ran her fingers through her gold hair and bit her lip as she nodded.

Belle smiled. "There's a man about town who can take care of that for us."

"For us?"

"You'll be back on your feet in a couple days."

Penny bit her lip. Belle didn't care for anything but the money her girls earned her. Penny and the others were livestock to her. Penny crossed her arms over her chest. "I want the baby."

Belle answered with a laugh as hollow as her sincerity. "It's the best thing for you."

Penny pointed her finger at Belle. "No, it's the best thing for you. You don't give a damn about what happens to us."

The madam cocked her head and gave Penny a crooked grin. "But, Penny, I do. If you don't go through with this, you might not have a warm place to stay the winter. Look outside and think how cold you and your baby'll be."

"I'll find someplace to go."

Belle grinned, flashing her three gold-capped teeth at Penny. "But where? No other house'll take you in this condition. No man'll marry you. You can save the child for a while, but you'll freeze before the spring thaw sets in."

"I want the baby."

"You don't even know whose it is, now do you?"

Penny sighed. Belle was right. How could she know whose it was? At least she could pretend it was the child of a man who loved her.

Belle sidled up to Penny and put her arm around her. "I can have it taken care of for you," she said. "I had it done five times and it never bothered me. It kept me out of work for a few days, but nothing more."

Penny shuddered at her words and at her touch. She shook her head. "I can't do it. I'm scared."

Belle patted her on the back. "Nothing to be scared of. It doesn't hurt more than that time of the month."

"No," she said, then clenched her jaw.

The madam dropped her arms from around Penny and shook her head. "Then get out." Belle pointed out the window. "See how long you'll survive in the cold."

"Give me the money you owe me."

Belle laughed. "I don't owe you a damn thing."

Penny felt a sudden desperation. Without money, she had no chance to survive. Who would take her in? "But half of everything I've made is mine. You know that. That's what we agreed to."

Belle shook her head. "That's what we agreed to as long as you stayed." Belle reached for Penny's hair and cupped the long, blonde curls in her sweaty palm. "Fair-haired girls like you bring a good price, Penny. That's why I took you on and offered you more than the other girls. If I'd had fair hair instead of this red mop, I'd be living in a mansion instead of running a house."

"You wouldn't be in a mansion if you hadn't been paid the share you were due."

"Get your baby fixed and stay until spring, then you'll get what you're due."

Penny bit her lip and shook her head. "I'm leaving."

Belle closed her fist around Penny's blonde hair and jerked it.

Penny cried out at the pain.

"Then you're leaving tonight. Gather what you can and get out." Belle slapped Penny across the face. "I'll send Buford to help you."

Penny paled at the mention of Buford, Belle's bouncer and live-in lover. He was as mean as Belle was heartless. Penny had heard stories of other women who had gotten pregnant while working for Belle. Those who had agreed to have their condition fixed always seemed luckier than those who didn't and Buford always seemed to be responsible for their bad luck. Buford punched one in the stomach, causing her to miscarry. He pushed another one down the stairs with the same result, compounded by a broken arm.

Belle waddled to the door, her jewelry rattling with each step. "I'll tell menfolk you're in an untoward state right now and I'll tell Buford. We'll miss your fair hair, Penny." She laughed as she opened the door. "I hope your child comes out okay."

The moment the door closed, Penny rushed to latch it. The latch would only keep Buford out for a moment at most, but any delay could make a difference.

Penny ripped her gown over her head, then bolted to her dresser, taking out drawers and a chemise to wear. Hurriedly, she jerked them on, then pulled out the warmest dress she had and jumped into it. Her fingers fumbled at the buttons as she ran around the bed to find the man's lace up boots she wore in cold or snowy weather.

Hearing footsteps in the hall, she didn't bother to tie the boots, but fell to her knees by the bed and retrieved the valise she had stored under the bed. The footsteps passed and she released a deep breath. Penny knew that if she could pack and slip into the parlor before Buford came to her room, she could at least get outside, for Buford wouldn't dare harm her in front of other men.

She dashed for the dresser and opened the top drawer, pulling her meager belongings and clothes out and stuffing them in the valise. She grabbed her Bible and the tintype of her dead parents from the dresser top and dropped them inside the valise, then snapped it shut. She tossed the case on her mattress, then bolted for the hook where her thick coat hung along with the wool shawl she used to cover her head. She grabbed the coat and shoved her arms inside, not taking time to button it. Then she jerked the shawl off the hook and draped it over her head as she dashed back to the bed. Lifting the corner of the mattress, she snatched her Remington Double Derringer and shoved it in her coat pocket.

As she picked up her valise, she realized how fast she was breathing and how hard her heart was pounding. She took a deep breath, trying to calm herself, then glanced out the window. Darkness had overtaken Silverton and she was glad because it would help her lose Buford if he gave chase. As she ran around the bed for the door, she knocked the washstand over, the porcelain wash basin and pitcher shattering on the wooden floor and splashing their contents upon her leg. She grabbed her gloves from the dresser, pulling one over her left hand and shoving the other in her teeth as she unlatched the door. Slowly, she poked her head out in the hallway and saw Buford slipping barefoot toward her.

A sadistic smile creased his faced. "I'm coming to help you."

She slammed the door, her fingers trembling as she latched it. She was trapped. Buford would knock the door down, then beat her, muffling her cries with her pillow.

Penny ran to the window, stumbling over the broken porcelain and falling to the floor beneath the windowsill. The valise flew from her hand and the glove fell from her teeth. Jumping to her feet, she heard Buford knock at the door.

"Let me in, Penny, I'm here to help."

She reached for the window and tried to shove it open, but the snow's moisture had swollen it tight. She could never open it.

Behind her, Buford pounded on the door. "Let me in."

"Just a minute," Penny stalled. "Let me get dressed."

Buford laughed. "I've seen you naked before."

"I'm coming," she called as she stepped to the end of the bed and picked up the overturned washstand. Taking a firm hold, she charged the window and flung the washstand through the muntins holding the four lower panes of glass in place. The wood bars broke and the glass shattered, leaving jagged edges around the sash.

"What the hell?" yelled Buford, pounding harder on the door.

Penny grabbed her valise and reached for her glove, just as Buford burst through the door.

"You bitch," he yelled, charging around the bed for her.

Penny abandoned the glove, tossing her valise outside.

Buford faltered when his bare feet stepped on the broken porcelain. He fell to the ground screaming, then scrambled to his hands and knees, crawling for Penny, his eyes wild with anger.

Penny screamed and dove out the window, feeling his hand brush against her boot for a moment. She felt a searing pain in the side of her calf, then landed in a cushion of snow. She clawed her way to her feet, then grabbed the valise and ran around the building, trying to find a place to hide. The soft snow, however, marked her every step and when she bent and grabbed her right calf, she felt a three-inch cut. Her hand came away sticky with blood. The tracks and blood would leave a trail even a blind man could follow.

Penny Heath didn't know where to go, she just knew she had to keep moving before Buford found his shoes and coat and came after her.

4

"You're a damn fool, Alf," announced Dick Pincham, lifting the patch and rubbing the scarred crater where his left eye had been before it was gouged out in a barroom fight four years before.

Agent Alfred Donner of the Animas Freight and Stage Company just grinned. "Hell, I'd say I was a genius."

Luther Perry stroked his red beard. "I was planning on spending some of that money during the winter."

"Yeah, me too," interjected Bibb Clack, holding his crooked nose indignantly in the air.

Donner strode around the freight counter and nodded. "That's what the sheriff would expect. He picked up enough of a trail in the snow to know you came into town. He'll spend the winter watching for fellows spending too much money. First thing you know, one of you'll be in jail and the money won't do any of us a bit of good."

Pincham replaced the patch. "The sheriff's not gonna think we killed our own men and took the payroll, now is he?"

Alf Donner licked his lips. "Think about it, Dick. Who but

17

us working for Animas Freight knew when the payroll was coming and who was bringing it?"

"How many genuine freight wagons carry an armed guard, genius?" Perry shot back.

"Yeah," Clack added.

"And now," said Pincham, scratching his head, "you want to turn the money over to that damn Blake Corley? Is that right, Alf?"

"He'll never know the difference. The way I figure it, we'll discard the bodies so no one'll find them, at least not until spring. Put the loot in their coffins and have Corley deliver them to Durango. My friend in Durango'll put up the coffins for the winter, then we can quit our jobs next spring and leave these parts twenty thousand dollars richer."

"Don't you mean twenty-five thousand dollars richer, Alf," Pincham challenged.

Donner shook his head. "My partner in Durango gets a share."

Perry eyed Donner skeptically. "How do we know Corley won't open the coffins?"

"Would you open a coffin?"

All three men shook their heads.

"What if he doesn't make it to Durango, Alf?" Pincham asked. "We'll lose all the money."

"If the sheriff catches us, we won't be able to spend it either. There's risks either way."

Perry licked his lips. "I'd sure like to spend a little of it before I let go of it."

Donner shook his head. "This was my idea from the beginning and you'll do what I say. We've been poor from the day we were born, but come spring we'll have all the spending money we need and we'll be spending it where folks won't be suspicious."

The trio around the stove grumbled among themselves.

"What happens if Corley doesn't make it, the wagon is

caught in a slide or something like that?" Pincham asked.

"Come spring, we'll find his remains and the coffins. It's as simple as that."

"I don't know, Alf," Pincham said.

"You don't have a choice. You do what I say if you want a cut and the first thing you'll do," Donner announced, "is hide the bodies before morning."

"Where?" Perry wanted to know.

"Take them up in the mountains and bury them under the snow."

"It don't seem right," Clack protested, "to do that to Barney and Pug."

"They don't care anymore," Donner responded. "Hell, you three are the ones who killed them."

Pincham nodded. "We had to in case they recognized us."

Donner stepped to the stove and held his hands toward the warmth. He looked at the two coffins in the corner. "They're dead and we're rich. Odd how life and death works out sometimes." He started to say more, but heard footsteps outside on the plank walk.

"It'll sit on my mind for a while, killing those two," Clack said.

"Hush, dammit," Donner said as the door swung open.

Clack's face paled with the fear that he might have been overheard. He breathed easier when he turned and saw a woman entering. She was an attractive woman bundled up against the cold. She stood barely five-feet six-inches tall. With a bare hand she removed a shawl from over her head as her gloved left hand dropped the valise at her feet. As she lifted her shawl, her light hair fell upon her shoulders. Her blue eyes seemed fearful. She was tentative as she studied the four men, then glanced in the corner at the coffins, before bending down and patting her right calf.

"I need a way out of town, fast. When's the next stage?"

"Spring, ma'am. Is that fast enough for you?" Donner replied, noting a dark stain on her dress and taking it for blood.

Her lip trembled.

"You haven't wintered in Silverton before, have you?"

She shook her head. "I arrived last spring."

"Say," Pincham said, standing up from his chair. "Don't you work down at Belle's."

She lowered her eyes. "Not any more."

"Oh, damn," said Donner. "If you left Belle's, I figure Buford won't be far behind. What is it? You pregnant or just tired of the trade?"

"What's it matter if there's no stage until spring?" she said with resignation.

"It's the difference between whether he beats you or kills you," Donner replied. "He's a mean one with women."

"We'd protect you from him, if you was willing to show us some favors," Perry offered.

"I'm quitting the trade," she replied. She bent to pick up her valise and turned for the door.

"Hold on a minute," said Donner. "There may be a freight wagon leaving tomorrow afternoon to take these bodies to Durango. You might be able to go along."

She smiled weakly. "Thanks."

"If Buford don't find you during the night," Pincham added.

The four men laughed as she disappeared out the door.

The air was bitter with the cold as Penny Heath hobbled away from the freight office, drawing the shawl back over her head. She went to two hotels, but she was turned away when she couldn't pay in advance. She wandered into the Federal Saloon, the thick smoke making her lightheaded, but she was cold and the room was warm.

Oblivious to the bartender who walked over, she jumped at his touch on her shoulder, spinning around, her free hand flying to her throat. Relieved that it was the bartender instead of Buford, she sighed. "You startled me."

The bartender had a kindly face. "You okay?"

Penny grimaced. What could she say?

"There's food on the bar, boiled potatoes, jerked beef and biscuits. You're welcome to a handful, even if you don't buy a drink."

"I don't have any money," she said, "and I'm not taking on men."

The bartender nodded. "I wasn't asking you to." The bartender pointed toward the bar, then reached to take her valise.

Penny held tight the handle. All she had in the world was packed in the valise.

The bartender smiled as his hand pried hers from the handle, then took her arm and escorted her to the bar. He lifted the valise to the counter and left it beside the bowls of food.

Penny took a potato and ate it hungrily. It was salty, but she was famished. The bartender placed a glass of water on the bar for her. "Thank you."

He nodded. "You look like you could use some help."

"There's a man after me."

"Why?"

"It doesn't matter. He'll just hurt me."

"Do you have a place to stay?"

She shook her head.

"There are beds upstairs. You're welcome to one."

"I'm not doing that, not any more I'm not."

The bartender reached across the bar and took her gloveless hand. "I'm not asking you to."

Penny pondered his offer. "Why you doing this?"

"I had a daughter once, but she died trying to birth my grandson. You remind me of her."

Tears welled in Penny's eyes and she looked away. "Do I look pregnant?"

"No," he answered, "just scared, like she looked before she died. Just think about the room. I'll see that no one bothers you." He released her hand and moved down the bar to attend a new customer who had blown through the door with a draft of wind that sent a chill down Penny's back. The bartender poured a beer for the new customer who looked to be a miner, then walked around the bar and checked the spittoons, picking up one and carrying it out the back door to empty it. He returned in a minute, shivering and shaking his head. "Wish I could bottle that and sell it in Texas during the summer. It'd make me a rich man."

"The tobacco juice?" Penny asked incredulously.

"No," the bartender laughed, "the cold."

Penny was about to answer when she felt the draft from the front door again. She looked over her shoulder, then gasped. Buford stood there licking his lips and pointing at her.

"I found you," he growled and started across the room.

Penny jerked her valise from the bar and flew past the bar toward the back door.

"Leave her alone," shouted the bartender in her wake.

Flinging the door open, she dashed out and ran as fast as her sore leg could carry her. She heard Buford's sinister laugh and then the sound of the back door slamming behind him.

She cut between two buildings, then ran back toward the street, hoping to lose Buford, but he seemed to be gaining on her. Her right leg hurt from the pain and the valise slowed her even further. "Help me," she screamed, but the streets were cold and empty. Nobody came.

Glancing over her shoulders, she saw Buford gaining on her. She turned between two buildings, but the valise slid from her fingers and she tripped over it, tumbling in the snow. She gasped first in pain, then in terror as Buford towered over her.

"You shouldn't of left Belle or taken with child," he huffed.

He made a fist with his right hand and pounded it into the palm of his left. "I intend to knock that baby right out of your gut, Penny."

In desperation, Penny tried to reach in her coat pocket for the Derringer, but the coat was tangled beneath her.

Buford kicked her. "Get up." He drew back to kick her again.

Penny braced for the full brunt of his boot in her belly. She gritted her teeth against the expected pain, then looked up when he failed to deliver the blow.

From somewhere a tall man had appeared, his face dark beneath the wide brim of his hat, and grabbed Buford by the arm, twisting it behind his back.

Penny scrambled to her feet, grabbing her valise and dashing away. "You okay, Missy?" came the voice of her benefactor. She didn't take time to answer. The last thing she heard was Buford's agonizing scream.

6

Moses Baldwin felt his luck had finally changed. In his pocket he carried a tobacco pouch of gold flakes and nuggets he had panned from a stream that fed into the Animas River upstream from Silverton. With a little more luck, Moses hoped he could file a claim and strike it rich before his thirty-fourth birthday. Not bad for a man born a slave in Alabama.

Through the snow, Moses trudged the mile from his primitive cabin to Silverton, timing his trip to arrive around dusk and just before the stores closed. At six-feet-four-inches tall and two hundred and thirty muscled pounds stretched taut within his coal-black skin, he was a conspicuous man, one of a dozen or less black men in Silverton but by far the biggest. Men knew him on sight, calling him "Black Baldy," which was better than some nicknames but not better than his own name. Moses could whip any three men in town, but was far too cautious to ever challenge a white man. He avoided trouble like a drunk avoids water. Moses had seen enough trouble back in Alabama during the War Between the States.

Moses arrived in Silverton late so he could buy his supplies just before the store closed and avoid running into the type of white man who judged a man by the blackness of his skin rather than the whiteness of his soul. Moses tugged the broad-brimmed hat over his forehead, pulled his coat tighter around his chest and adjusted on his neck the empty flour sack he used as a muffler. On the trip back to his cabin, he would use the flour sack to tote his supplies. Though he kept a rifle at his cabin, he didn't own a sidearm, figuring a pistol could get a black man in more trouble than it could get him out of.

The streets were virtually empty when Moses reached Silverton. That always reduced the chance of trouble. He went to the mercantile he frequented and loaded his flour sack with a dozen canned goods, a hunting knife, a loaf of bread baked that morning, two extra pairs of woolen socks, a new pair of gloves, and a box of cartridges for his rifle.

He settled up with the merchant, then retreated outside. He figured he should walk back home, but he had a hankering for a drink. Moses didn't frequent saloons because some drunk always seemed to want to whip him because of his size or the color of his skin. Some saloons were icier than the weather to blacks, but there was one that allowed Moses to enter by the back door and take his drinks in the back storage room.

Toting the flour sack over his shoulder, Moses walked down the street then circled the saloon. He recognized the sign and wished he knew the name of the establishment, but he could not read and he didn't dare ask anyone what the sign said. Once it was known a man couldn't read, some thieves tried to take by legal paper what they couldn't take by force. Moses rapped on the back door.

Shortly, the door swung open and the bartender grinned. "Howdy, Moses, come on in."

Moses took off his hat and nodded. "Hope I ain't troubling you none too much."

"Why, Moses, you're never a bother and you're welcome here anytime, whether you want to sit out front or stay back here."

"Here's fine. I like my solitude."

The bartender had a kindly face and a decent soul. "Want me to light a lamp?"

"No need for that, sir. I don't need much light to eat or drink."

The bartender pointed him to the corner where a couple whiskey barrels bracketed a wobbly table and a chair with a broken leg wired in place. "That chair's unsteady. A man your size should sit in it real easy."

Moses nodded as he edged toward the table, dropped his flour sack atop it, removed his hat, unbuttoned his coat and settled gingerly down on the chair. The bartender departed, returning minutes later with a mug of beer and a plate of boiled potatoes, jerked beef, and cold biscuits.

"Anything more you need, you just holler," the bartender said as he backed away and returned to the bar.

Before taking a bite of food or a sip of beer, Moses dug into his britches pocket and extracted a coin to pay for the refreshment. He left it on the edge of the table, then attacked the food, enjoying it in spite of its saltiness.

Through the thin wood wall, he could make out fragments of conversation among the dozen or so men who were soaking up the saloon's liquor as well as its warmth. Like them, Moses lingered, spending more than an hour and a half on three mugs of beer and a second helping of food. Every time he seemed ready to make the march to his cabin, someone would open the front door and Moses could feel the wind's icy fingers all the way in the back room. Each time he decided he could stay a bit longer before heading home.

Once the bartender came through with a spittoon and carried it out the back door to dump it. When the bartender returned, Moses figured he had delayed the inevitable as long as he could. He stood up, buttoned his coat, picked up his hat, then snugged it down tight over his head. Moses sighed at the thought of the cold walk. As he was picking up his burlap sack of supplies, he heard a commotion in the front of the saloon.

Suddenly a woman with a valise in her hand dashed through the back room, flung open the rear door and disappeared into the cold. She was followed by the bartender, then another, bigger man.

"Leave her alone," the bartender cried.

With a hard slap with the back of his hand, the man knocked the bartender aside, then jumped out the back door. Moses's temper flared and he knocked the chair over as he rushed to the bartender, who waved him away.

"I'm okay, I'm okay," he said.

Moses nodded. "I'll get him for you."

"Protect the girl."

With the sack in his hand, he darted through the door, slamming it in his wake. Then he turned the direction the assailant had taken and caught a glimpse of him darting between two buildings. Moses gave chase, moving quickly with muscled strides. He followed the assailant out onto the deserted main street, then saw him dart between two buildings on the other side.

Moses sprinted toward the snow-shrouded structures, then turned between them. In the soft night glow of the snow he saw the man towering over the woman. The bully kicked her. Moses dropped his flour sack and crept up behind the preoccupied man who drew back his foot to kick the woman again. Moses grabbed the man's arm before he could loose his boot for the woman's stomach.

The man was strong and he resisted, but Moses was powerful. He twisted the man's arm behind his back. The man gasped in pain as the woman scrambled to her feet. She grabbed her valise and ran.

"You okay, Missy?" Moses called.

The woman disappeared around the building, saying nothing, though Moses thought he heard her sobbing.

The bully resisted Moses' powerful grip, but Moses lifted the bent arm behind the man's back until he screamed.

"Why you threatening Missy?"

The bully refused to answer.

Moses jerked his arm higher. "What's your name?"

"Buford," the man gasped.

"Leave Missy alone."

Buford glanced over his shoulder and saw Moses for the first time.

"You're not ordering me around, nigger."

Moses shook his head. "Ought not to've called me that." Moses shoved Buford's arm up to his shoulder blade. Buford screamed with pain, then screamed again when the arm cracked.

Buford gasped. "I'll see the law gets you."

Moses shoved Buford to the ground, then stood over him. "Don't go beating up ladies."

"She wasn't a lady. She was a whore." Buford winced as he tried to straighten his bent and broken right arm. His face contorted in pain.

Seeing Buford's left hand sliding toward his right hip, Moses bent over him and pulled the pistol from his holster.

"Bastard," Buford scowled.

With the pistol Moses slugged Buford across his temple. The bully went limp in the snow.

Moses tucked the pistol in his coat pocket then moved to retrieve his sack of supplies. Though he knew he had done nothing wrong, he felt relieved when he saw the street remained empty. Some people didn't take to a black man whipping a white one, no matter if he deserved it.

Moses retreated to the saloon and knocked on the back door.

"Who is it?" called the bartender from inside.

"Moses Baldwin."

The door cracked slightly and Moses saw the bartender eyeing him before opening it wide enough to let Moses in.

"Is the girl okay?" the bartender asked.

Moses shrugged. "I never got the chance to ask Missy. The fellow after her'll be stoved up for a bit, a broken arm and a bad headache."

"Thanks for protecting her." The bartender dug in his britches pocket and pulled out a coin. "Take it."

Moses hesitated, but the bartender grabbed his massive hand and dropped the coin in his palm. "Food and drinks are on me tonight for you looking after that girl."

"You know Missy?"

The bartender clenched his lips and shook his head. "She just reminds me of someone I once knew."

"Thank you, sir. I best be getting back to my cabin."

"You could stay the night upstairs."

Moses shook his head. "The law might not take kindly to a black man assisting, Missy. I best be going."

"Remember you're always welcome here, Moses. You can even sit out front if you like."

"Thank you, sir," Moses answered, then turned and started the mile walk toward his cabin.

Though he knew he should head straight for his cabin, he worried for the young woman he had rescued and spent an hour wandering down Silverton's wide streets, searching for her. She seemed helpless as a kitten.

Failing to find her, he turned toward his cabin well after midnight. The clouds were thick and low over the mountains. Moses crossed the wide clearing where Silverton had arisen and entered the trees, taking the most direct route back to his cabin. His mind gradually grew numb from the cold and he lost track of how far he had walked. Then from somewhere out of the murkiness he heard cursing voices. He didn't think much of it until he walked up on three men.

He froze in his tracks, knowing that men out this time of night could be up to no good. Then he realized two of the men were carrying a body toward a shallow grave. He began to back away, but stepped on a downed branch beneath the snow. The branch snapped and the three men glanced toward him.

"What the hell?" yelled a man who looked to be wearing an eye patch.

"It's Black Baldy," cried another.

"Get him," yelled the first again.

One man swatted at his pistol beneath his heavy coat and the other two dropped the body and went for the rifles propped against the trees.

Moses turned and ran.

Gunshots exploded through the stillness.

Moses wasn't sure what he had stumbled upon except that three men were trying to hide the bodies of two murder victims.

Men like that would think nothing of killing a third man. And, they knew who he was. One of them had called him "Black Baldy."

If they didn't find him by dawn, they would know where he lived and find him at his cabin. Moses ran for his life, uncertain where to go or where to turn. All he knew was his life wasn't worth a plugged nickel anymore. His luck has turned as rancid as spoiled meat. The way he figured it, the trio of killers would blame him for murdering their two victims and by morning all of Silverton would be looking to hang him.

7

"What do you mean he got away?" yelled Alfred Donner still wiping the sleep from his eyes. "I told you not to let anybody see you."

"How was we to know Black Baldy'd be wandering about in the middle of the night?" Dick Pincham growled as he lit a lamp.

The room was washed in the lamp's yellow light as Alfred Donner threw the covers off his bed in the back of the freight office and sat up in his union suit. "From the beginning, now, tell me everything that happened."

Pincham nodded. "While you was sleeping in a warm bed, Alf, we were out there freezing our tails off burying Barney and Pug."

"Yeah," echoed Luther Perry. "Why weren't you out helping us?"

Alf scowled. "If I had been, nobody'd slipped up on us, I know that for certain."

Pincham cursed. "We'd dug the graves and were loading Barney into one when Black Baldy appeared out of nowhere. He stood there watching us for I don't know how long before we saw him. Then we fired at him and gave chase, but he got away."

"Damn," Alf said. "You certain it was Black Baldy?"

"Ain't that many fellows in these parts as big as him," said Perry.

"Or as black," added Bibb Clack, wiping the tip of his crooked nose.

"Did he recognize any of you?"

"Who's to know?" Pincham replied.

"We damn sure better know or we could be fit with a hangman's noose," Donner shot back. Pondering his options, Donner paced back and forth across his small sleeping quarters. "We've got to kill him before he tells the sheriff."

"Hell, Alf, you think we ain't smart enough to figure that out?" Pincham said, slamming his fist atop Alf's rolltop desk. "Why do you think we looked for him for an hour before returning to finish burying Barney and Pug?"

Donner waved off Pincham's protest. "We know who it was. He may or may not know who you three are." Donner rubbed his chin in contemplation.

"Maybe we shouldn't send the payrolls off," Clack offered.

"All the more reason to now," Donner replied. "Even if Black Baldy goes to the sheriff, the sheriff won't believe him until he sees the bodies." Donner clapped his hands. "That's it."

"What's it?" Perry asked.

"The way I figure it, Baldwin's only got three choices. He can go to the sheriff, forget he ever saw anything and go to his cabin or try to leave town." Donner paced back and forth in front of his bed.

"So what?" Perry interrupted.

Donner grinned. "Guess you boys'll have to stand watch for a day or so. One at the graves. If Black Baldy brings the sheriff out to look around, kill them both. One of you needs to watch his cabin, kill him if he shows up there and one of you needs to watch the road to Durango in case he tries to head south for low country."

"Only a fool would try to get to Durango now that the snows have started."

"A fool or someone scared for his life."

Pincham crossed his arms over his chest. "And just what the hell'll you be doing while we're standing watch?"

"Handling company business as usual. Wasn't me that got spotted with the bodies," Donner answered. "It'll look suspicious if we close the freight office until we kill the darkie." Donner pointed to the corner. "You boys better grab a couple blankets and buffalo robes to take with you. It may get cold before you find your new friend."

The three men grumbled, then marched to the corner, each grabbing a couple blankets and a buffalo robe that the company loaned coach passengers during cold or damp weather.

"Who's going where?" Donner inquired.

Pincham spoke first. "I'll take his cabin. He's bound to show up there."

"I'll watch the graves," Perry said.

Donner looked at Clack. "Looks like you'll cover the road."

Clack shrugged.

"Take your rifles with you," Donner commanded, "and don't let anyone see you this time."

As the men slipped out the back door into the cold, Donner turned to watch them through the rear window, but it was frosted over. He blew out the lamp and fell back on his bed, cursing the bad luck that had befallen his plan. He questioned whether he should remove the strong boxes he had already secured inside the coffins. A hundred thousand dollars was a lot of money to turn blindly over to a man so desperate to get out of Silverton that he would challenge the icy winter roads all the way down to Durango, a three-thousand-foot drop from Silverton.

It was a risk, no question about it, but Donner figured it was riskier not to get the money out of Silverton. He thought about his decision until dawn, then got up and added wood to the stove and warmed up the freight office. He fixed a pot of coffee to get him started until the eatery opened across the street. When he saw the cook unlock the door, he grabbed his coat and ran over, gobbling down a quick breakfast of ham, potatoes, biscuits and jam, then returning to the freight office. Just as he opened the door, he heard his name called from down the walk.

Turning in the direction of the call, he froze. It was Sheriff Stewart Johnson. "Morning, Stew," he managed, until he caught his composure.

Johnson tugged on the end of his handlebar mustache like he always did when he was thinking. The sheriff was a lean man with narrow eyes and quick snake-like movements. He hated nonsense like a preacher hates sin and rumor had it he was known to laugh on occasion, but no one in Silverton had ever witnessed such an outburst.

"Anything new on the murders?" Donner asked.

Clenching his jaw, Johnson shook his head. "The bastards are bound to still be in town. If they're thinking of waiting out the winter, I'll still be watching for them to slip up and spend a little too much money or let word slip in one of the bordellos."

"Then what brings you here this early in the morning?" Donner waited in the doorway for an answer.

Johnson motioned for Donner to move inside. "We can talk about it inside, where it's warm."

Donner took a deep breath, then stepped into the freight office, closing the door after the sheriff marched through. Wordlessly, both men stepped to the stove and held their hands toward it.

"Now what was it you wanted, Stew?"

The sheriff rubbed his hands together. "You familiar with Moses Baldwin, the one some call Black Baldy?"

Donner swallowed hard and nodded. "Seems I've heard of him. What about him?"

"Some trouble last night he was involved in."

The freight agent let out a slow breath.

"Seems Baldwin whipped Belle Farthing's old man, Buford. At least that's what Buford says. I don't know that I trust a man who beats up on fallen women and lives off a madam like Belle."

Donner shook his head. "Can't say that I've seen him."

"I thought you might have seen him. I saw your lamp on late last night. Stay on the lookout for him. Now that the snow's started, I don't guess you'll have as much to do seeing as how the freight and passenger business is slowing up with the snow."

"I've got one more wagon I want to get to Durango."

"What's the need?"

Donner pointed to the two coffins in the corner. "It's the least I can do for Pug and Barney, get them to their families."

"Who you sending, Pincham or Perry?"

Donner didn't answer for a moment.

"Don't tell me it's Clack. He couldn't drive a thirsty horse to water."

"No, none of them want to leave until you find out who killed Barney and Pug. There's a miner named Blake Corley that's agreed to get them to Durango."

"It'll be a tough road. You know that, Alf."

"It's the least we can do for Barney and Pug."

8

Stiff and cold, Blake Corley emerged from the tunnel where he had spent the night. The midmorning sun had broken through the clouds and the snow glistened with a blinding brilliance. Blake shielded his eyes as he marched to his blackened cabin site. He remembered leaving the lamp lit and building a fire in the stove when he left for town and he wondered which had started the fire. His cabin, like his dreams of wealth, had been reduced to ashes. There was nothing left, not even a blanket he would need on the trip to Durango, but he no longer cared. He was going to get to Durango, even if he had to walk all the way, even if it killed him. Dying was better than going crazy in Silverton.

He stepped away from his cabin and without looking back at the charred remnants or at Anvil Mountain, he marched down the slope toward town. He squinted against the glare reflecting from the snow and stumbled as he tried to kick the kinks and cramps out of his leg muscles. Blake tramped through the snow which was still soft and powdery, but the sun would melt enough of it that once sundown came the snow would glaze over with a film of ice, making walking difficult.

He approached the freight and stage office a little before noon. Stepping on the plank walk, he stomped the snow and mud off his boots, then entered, pausing to see who was sitting around the stove. He saw a comely woman with wide, blue eyes and a valise in her lap, but not the three men who had tormented him for buying the Haney claim. Relieved, he tipped his hat at the woman and approached the counter.

"Alf Donner," he called, staring at the two coffins in the corner.

Emerging from the back, Donner nodded at Blake. "Hear your cabin burned down."

Blake nodded.

"You've had as bad a run of lousy luck as any man I've known in these parts. I don't know that I can trust a wagon and team to you, not with such a precious cargo." Donner looked to the corner. "God rest their souls."

"I can make it to Durango."

"Are you the one going to Durango?" called a soft voice behind him.

Blake turned around to see the blue-eyed young woman arise from her chair.

"Sit down, girlee," ordered Donner. "I'll tell you when you can talk to him."

The young lady shook her head, her yellow tresses spilling over her shoulder as she sat down and placed the valise in her lap.

Blake felt sorry for her as he turned to face Donner.

"Do you still want the bodies taken to Durango or not? If not, let me know now so I can start walking and get a good jump before night falls."

Donner scratched his chin. "You sure you know how to drive a team?"

Blake nodded. "Handled a two-mule team back in Kansas."

"This is six mules and this ain't no Kansas road. It's a downhill grade on an icy cliff road. The road's narrow in places with no more than inches for error. It's damn sure not as wide as Kansas."

Grimacing, Blake turned around and started for the door.

"Where you going?" Donner called.

"Durango. I figure I'll be there by the time you quit your jawing."

As Blake passed the stove, the woman dropped her valise and jumped up.

"Please, don't leave without the wagon—and me."

Blake looked at the woman. "Nobody but a fool would make the trip now. You heard him."

"Please," she pleaded, "take me with you." Her eyes welled with tears. "I'll not last the winter here. I have no place to turn."

Donner emerged from behind the counter and strode to Blake. "I'll trust you to take the two coffins. Hell, you can't kill them." Donner laughed at his joke.

Blake pointed at the woman. "Do I have to take her?"

Donner shrugged. "It's up to you. She might come in handy to keep you warm at night."

"He doesn't mean that, ma'am," Blake said, taking off his hat.

"Sure I do. She ain't nothing but a whore."

Blake felt his face flush, embarrassed at the woman's shame. He reached out and touched her hand. "Nothing against you, ma'am, but I couldn't risk your life in unpredictable weather."

"There's a man out to kill me. I risk my life staying here."

Donner laughed. "She's probably taken too much laudanum and it's warped her mind. I don't care, Corley, if you take her or not, as long as you get her out of here for the time being and get these two coffins to Durango safe and sound."

Blake pointed out the window to the eatery across the street. "Maybe we can go there and talk about it, ma'am."

"Penny Heath's my name." She dabbed at the corner of her eyes with her sleeve.

"You two just do that," Donner said. "It'll take me a couple hours to load up the coffins, secure them, and harness the team. I figure you'll want to leave today. Weather being unpredictable as it is, you'll need to get as far along as you can."

Blake nodded and stepped to the chair to retrieve Penny's valise.

She smiled as he took her arm and guided her to the door. They emerged into the snowy glare and walked across the muddy street to the eatery. Inside they took a table in the back corner.

"What do you want?" he asked.

"Nothing. I don't have any money."

"I don't have much, either, but enough for us both to have a meal."

"Please, you don't have to do that, just let me go with you to Durango."

"It's dangerous. You heard Donner."

She nodded. "A man's trying to kill me. Might have done so last night, but some man roughed him up first. I got away, but he'll find me. You've got to take me."

Blake detected desperation in her voice. "I'll have enough to watch for without having to look out for a woman. Besides, the nights will be bitter cold."

"I didn't have a place to stay last night. I slept outside as best I could and I survived."

"No, I just can't let you take the risk."

A tear slid down Penny's cheek. "Is it because I'm a whore?"

"No, no, just that I'd hate to see something happen to you."

"You won't do it?"

"I can't."

Penny began to sob.

Blake felt helpless before her tears and embarrassed when the cook approached their table.

"What'll it be," he said, staring at Penny.

Blake stared at the menu written on a chalkboard on the

wall. "Give us both a bowl of stew, some cornbread, and plenty of hot coffee."

The cook nodded, then retreated to the kitchen.

"It's because I'm a whore."

"It's nothing to do with you being anything but a woman."

Penny looked up from her hands, her eyes watering, her lips trembling. "Please, take me. If they don't kill me, they'll at least kill my child. I'm pregnant."

Blake shook his head, then pinched the bridge of his nose between his two fingers. He didn't know what to say. He dropped his hands to the table. "You're carrying a child? You shouldn't travel."

"Please," she said, reaching for his hand and placing hers atop it.

The soft flesh of her palm felt warm against his callused and scarred hand. How could he say no, but how could he say yes?

"I don't have money. I don't have anything to offer except what other men have paid for. I will give you that, if you'll just take me with you, please."

Again Blake shook his head, not in answer to her question but in frustration about what to do.

"Don't you find me a little bit pretty? Find us a room and I'll start paying you before we go."

"Okay, I mean yes, I mean no." Blake was as confused as he'd ever been. "I'll take you to Durango."

Penny patted his hands. "There's a saloon down the street, a kindly bartender said I could sleep there. I can take you there, make good on my offer before we leave."

"No, Penny. You can go with me. You don't have to do anything like that."

"Thank you." She squeezed his hand. "If you change your mind about, you know, just tell me and I'll make room for you in my blanket."

Blake let out a slow breath, relieved when the cook finally brought their stew.

They ate slowly and silently, neither knowing what to say or how to say it. Blake had a second bowl of stew, then ordered slices of apple pie and more coffee. Penny didn't eat her pie, pushing it across the table for Blake to have.

Blake had avoided looking at Penny after her desperate offer, but the next time his gaze met hers, he was pleased to see a sparkle in her blue eyes. He had to admit she was a comely woman. Were circumstances different, he would be proud to go anywhere with her on his arm.

They lingered at the table even after they finished their meal for they had time to kill. Neither seemed to know what to say and their awkward gazes seldom met. When Blake finally paid for the meal, she thanked him.

They spent another thirty minutes at the table until they saw a six-team freight wagon pull up in front of the freight office and Alfred Donner jump down from the seat to the ground.

"Maybe we should go on," Blake said.

She nodded.

"It's a long way to Durango."

"But at least I'll be going there," she said.

9

Alfred Donner pointed to the toolbox on the side of the freight wagon. "There's a shovel, an ax, a crosscut saw, and other tools inside. You should be good for everything except a broken axle."

Next he lifted a corner of the tarp for Blake Corley to see the two coffins strapped to the wagon bed. "Up front there's four blankets and two buffalo robes, in case she gets the urge to rut."

Blake coughed, hoping Penny didn't hear the insult, then knotted his fist and fought the urged to slug Donner.

"There's a couple bags of grub, some jerky, a few cans of food, some crackers, and a tin of matches. It should be enough to get you to Durango, unless you have trouble. Then you're on your own."

"We'll make do."

"You do that, Corley." Donner pulled the tarp taut over the sideboard and tied it over the tailgate. "When you get to Durango, take the coffins to the freight agent there, Ray Turpin is his name. He'll see that the families are notified. Then you're on your own."

Blake nodded and turned toward the mule team, Donner walking step for step with him.

"You sure you want to go through with this, Corley? I don't want you abandoning the wagon and riding the mules into Durango."

"I don't have much any more," Blake said, "but I still have my word and it's good as gold."

Blake gave Penny a hand and helped her get footing on a wheel spoke. Then he assisted her as she stepped into the driver's box. Blake saw a patch of bare skin on her calf and a wound caked with dried blood.

Penny modestly covered her calf with her dress, then settled on the bench seat.

Blake boosted himself up into the driver's box and sat down beside her. He untied the reins with his gloved hands, released the brake lever and whistled as he shook the reins. The mules lifted their heads, then the wagon lurched forward, bound for Durango.

"Remember," yelled Donner, "this ain't Kansas. Don't get your brake too hot on the downhill slope or you'll wind up dropping over some cliff and swimming in the Animas River."

Blake shook the reins again, anxious to get away from Alfred Donner and Silverton.

Thin clouds had drifted over the mountains since lunch and the glare on the snow was not nearly as bad as it had been earlier. He took a deep breath, the cold air searing his lungs, and rode wordlessly to the edge of town, not knowing what to say to Penny. Out of the corner of his eye, he saw a soft smile on her face and realized how pretty she was when she wasn't worried. He noticed her rubbing her bare right hand with her gloved hand.

"Lose your glove?"

She nodded.

"How'd you hurt your leg?"

Her smile evaporated as her lips tightened.

"You don't have to tell me."

"I jumped out a window. The glass cut me."

"You scared?"

"Not now, now that we're leaving Silverton and I'm with you."

Blake laughed. "I'm just a dumb Kansas sodbuster that thought he could strike it rich mining. I was wrong. I figured I'd go crazy waiting out the winter. I came up here with more than five hundred dollars. Now I've barely got enough to pay for our lunch."

"You've still got your good name."

"That ain't much."

"It's more than I've got." Penny looked off to the side.

Blake didn't try to respond. He just removed the glove from his right hand and offered it to her. "This'll keep your fingers warm."

"Don't you need it?"

He shook his head. "I've got a better feel for the reins without it."

Her hand brushed against his as she took the glove. She slid it over her hand, then lifted her shawl to cover her hair and screen her face.

As they passed the last building on the road, Blake saw a man atop a bay horse angling to cut him off. Blake drew back on the lines as the rider reined up his mount in the middle of the road.

Penny squirmed on the seat. "It's the sheriff."

Blake nodded.

Silently, the sheriff approached, studying the mules, then Blake, Penny, and the wagon. Drawing up beside Blake, he tipped his hat. "Evening Miss Penny, sorry to see you leaving town, you being a more decent sort among your type."

Uncertain whether to consider that an insult or compliment of Penny, Blake removed his hat. "How can we help you, Sheriff?"

"You must be Blake Corley, the one that bought the Haney claim."

"Seems that's what I'm known for in these parts."

"That's not the most foolish thing you've ever done, Corley."

Blake cocked his head and stared at the lawman. "Then what was the most foolish thing I ever did, Sheriff."

"Drive a wagon out of Silverton after the snows have set in."

"You can't stop us."

"I could, but not legally. You mind if I search your wagon?"

"Why?"

"Well, Corley, this very wagon was robbed of a goodly amount of money two days ago. I figure whoever stole it would like to get it out of town where they could spend it without being too obvious."

"We didn't rob nobody."

"Now, Corley, I didn't say you did."

"There's nothing back there but a couple coffins and a few supplies to get us to Durango."

Johnson nudged his horse toward the back of the wagon. "I'll just take a look see."

Blake sat the brake and wrapped the lines around the brake lever as the sheriff passed. Dismounting, the lawman tied the bay's reins to the rear wheel, then untied the tarp and flung it back. He climbed into the wagon bed, checked the sacks of food, the buffalo robes, and the blankets.

"You just as well take a look in the coffins, while you're at it, Sheriff."

Penny groaned at the suggestion.

Johnson shook his head. "I helped lay them both out. I don't figure they'd up and walk away."

"Did you check their pockets first?" Blake asked.

Johnson's taut face grew tighter as he climbed out of the wagon, snugged the tarp back in place, then checked the tool-box. "Whoever murdered them wouldn't think twice about killing you." He dropped the lid on the toolbox, then untied the reins of his bay. He mounted and rode around to Penny's side of the wagon.

"Miss Penny, you wouldn't know anything about Buford getting beat up last night, now would you? A few men reported seeing him chasing you out of the Federal Saloon. He was found with his arm broken and a knot the size of a tater across the side of his head."

Penny shook her head. "I didn't do it, Sheriff."

Johnson nodded. "Damn shame you couldn't have given him what he deserved, but Buford said a big black man, one they call Black Baldy, done it to him. You don't know Moses Baldwin do you?"

"No, sir."

"Good enough, Miss Penny." Johnson tipped his hat to her again. "I'll let you two be riding. I hope you make it. You weren't cut out for the profession, Miss Penny. Glad to see you're leaving it."

She smiled.

Blake unwrapped the reins, released the brake, and started the mules to pulling the freight wagon again. He studied the road ahead, occasionally glancing at Penny.

The basin that cradled Silverton gradually narrowed into a canyon and valley that followed the Animas River to Durango. The trees reached the edge of the road, then began to climb the surrounding mountains. As they neared the mouth of the canyon, the rush of the Animas's noisy waters reached their ears. Gradually, the river took up most of the narrowing canyon floor, leaving only a slender ledge for a road. As the wagon rattled down the road, Blake was startled to hear gunshots up the mountain slope. He twisted in his seat and scanned the snow-covered slope as the wagon moved around a bend in the road. Blake heard a shout and then saw a large man run from the cover of the trees toward the mules.

The man carried a gun in his hand. He was big and he was black.

Blake reached beneath his coat to pull his own revolver.

"No," yelled Penny, grabbing Blake's hand. "I think he's a friend."

10

After Moses Baldwin had finally given his three pursuers the slip, he had retreated to Silverton. It would have been foolish to hide in the mountains or among the trees because his footprints in the snow would have led the trio right to him. At least in Silverton, his footprints would mingle with those of everyone else until he could figure what to do.

But those three men weren't his only problem. If the man whose arm he had broken had gone to the sheriff, the law would be looking for him as well. In Silverton he would be as easy to spot as soot upon the snow. Moses cursed his luck for stumbling upon those three murderers. At least his luck was better than that of the two men they were burying. At least, so far.

Moses walked down the middle of Silverton's dark and deserted streets until he was certain his trail could no longer be picked up, then he skulked between a couple buildings, looking for a place to hide. He found a woodshed and slipped inside, dropping his sack of goods on the shed's earthen floor. He leaned against the plank wall for a moment, then slid down to the floor, sitting with knees bent and his arms wrapped around his legs to hold what little warmth he felt. Gradually, he dozed off.

When he finally awoke, he squinted against the glare shining between the cracks of the shed's grayed wood. Figuring it midmorning, maybe later, he arose and peeked through the cracks between the planks. He could make out the freight office as well as other buildings up and down the street. He grumbled about his predicament, then slumped back against the wall, considering his options.

The three men he had seen hiding the bodies knew who he was. If they knew that, they would know where he lived. Moses figured they were watching his cabin, just waiting for him to return home so they could ambush him.

There were hazards in going to the sheriff. The three murderers could already have visited the sheriff and said *they* had stumbled upon *him* hiding the bodies. Who would the sheriff believe, three white men or a single black man? Also, even if the trio hadn't gone to the sheriff, the man whose arm Moses had broken during the night might have. Moses couldn't deny he was the one who had whipped the fellow, even if the man deserved it.

Moses figured he could steal a horse, though that might not be easy, most folks having already sent their animals to low country before the deep snows came. There would certainly be a few mules and maybe even a horse or two in the stables behind the freight office, but stealing a mount would only add one more crime to the list he could possibly face.

Moses patted his coat pocket, glad to have the pistol he had taken from the man he had beaten. He toyed with the flour sack, glad to have a few supplies to carry him a few days, if necessary. He pulled the loaf of bread and the new hunting knife and scabbard from the sack and sliced off a hunk of bread. Though cold, the bread sated the cravings in his stomach. He was tempted to eat more, but he resisted, shoving the loaf back in the sack. The bread and the tinned goods were all the supplies he had for the foreseeable future. He slid the knife back in its scabbard, then unbuttoned his coat and slipped the scabbard over his belt and around to the middle of his back where he preferred to wear it.

He figured if he waited much longer, he would be discovered by the first person who came for wood. He was running out of time and options. Grabbing his sack of supplies, he straightened as much as he could in the low-roofed shed. Through the cracks between the planks, he saw something that gave him hope.

The freight agent was harnessing up a team of mules. That meant he would be sending a freight wagon out of town, most likely south to Durango. Moses knew if he could make it to the mouth of the canyon road, he could hide among the rocks and trees until the wagon approached. Then he could hitch a ride on the wagon.

His only problem would be getting from town without being seen. Moses pulled the brim of his hat down over his forehead until it reached his eyebrows. He bent the rear brim of the hat to cover as much of his neck and ears as he could, then turned up his coat collar.

With sack in hand he slipped out of the woodshed, squinting at the brilliant glare angling off the snow. The glare brought tears to his eyes and he cursed it mightily until he realized that the blinding reflection made it just as hard for anyone else to see him. The glare was his ally in getting out of town undetected. He moved quickly from the shed to the nearest dwelling, then strode swiftly from building to building, glancing periodically behind him and to each side.

A few folks were about, handling their business, but most stayed inside out of the cold. When he finally slipped away from town, he jogged across the clearing that funneled down into the canyon road which paralleled the river to Durango. Each breath turned to a cloud of vapor as he exhaled. The cold air dug deep into his lungs as he traversed the broad clearing, then angled up the broad shoulder of the mountain abutting the road. Once among the trees, the glare was not nearly so severe and Moses opened his eyes more fully.

Moses climbed some three hundred feet up the slope until he found a spot overlooking the first bend in the road. He found a spot that could screen him, yet still allow him a view of town and the road. He brushed the snow from a rock and sat down, leaning against the trunk of a pine tree. He watched and waited, all the while wondering if he had misread the freight agent's intentions. Gradually, a veil of clouds drifted across the mountains, taking the bite out of the glare and giving him a better view of Silverton. He was relieved when he finally saw the agent drive the team to the front of the freight office where a pair of drivers climbed aboard. Moses stood up from his rock, grabbed his flour sack, and waited until the freight wagon started for the river road. Moses laughed to himself, then angled down the mountain away from Silverton, planning to stop the wagon around the bend, out of view from the town.

He moved hurriedly, not worrying about the noise he made as he ran through the trees. He was about halfway to the road when he realized his carelessness was dumb. The sound of an unexpected voice confirmed the hazard of his recklessness.

"So there you are, you black son of a bitch," came the voice.

Moses spun around and saw a man, not fifty feet away in a den of snow-covered rocks, pointing a rifle straight at his chest.

"We figured you'd try to leave town," he laughed.

Moses gauged the man. He was small with a crooked nose and wild eyes.

"I waited all night in the cold for you," he said, emerging from his rock fortress. "Damn near froze to death. If there's a way I could kill you more than once, I'd sure do it."

"What did I do?"

"You seen something you shouldn't have."

"Maybe you done something you shouldn't've done," Moses replied, calculating his chances of charging the man and overpowering him.

The gunman lifted the rifle to his shoulder.

Moses knew he would die trying to reach the gunman. Instead, he turned and scampered away jumping between trees and rocks.

The man's curse followed him along with the sound of his rifle discharging.

Moses flinched at the sound. The bullet thudded into a tree overhead. Moses darted up the hill, using whatever trees and rocks he could for cover. Another shot clipped a small branch that fell in his face. Moses swatted the branch away, then stumbled, dropping his supplies, and fell, just as a shot sliced through the space where he had been standing.

Scrambling to his knees he grabbed his supply sack and lunged up the slope, his legs churning in the snow. He must devise a ploy or he would surely die. He saw a large boulder downslope and darted in that direction for cover.

As he neared the rock, another errant shot rang out.

Moses staggered as if he had been hit, then stumbled forward, throwing his sack of supplies. He twisted around, grabbing his chest, then fell backwards behind the boulder.

Moses gritted his teeth as he hit the ground, hoping that his assassin would fall for his ploy.

"Got you, you son of a bitch," the man shouted.

Moses turned over, then crouched ready to spring on his assailant.

The gunman jumped around the rock to examine his kill.

The look of sadistic glee on his face turned to terror as Moses lunged like a panther for him, knocking him down and grabbing his rifle. Both men fought for the gun, but Moses was bigger, quicker, and stronger. He ripped the weapon from his assailant's hands.

The man let out a desperate cry then managed to find his feet, but Moses shoved the rifle at his boots, tripping him. The man tumbled down slope, then slammed into a tree.

Moses jumped to his feet and charged the man before he

could get his bearings. Moses cracked the rifle butt against the man's head. He groaned for a moment, then went limp. Quickly, Moses ripped open the man's coat, unbuckled his gun belt and jerked it from under him.

Hurriedly, Moses retreated to the boulder, grabbed his sack of supplies, shoved the gun belt inside, then charged down the slope, angling across the mountain to catch the freight wagon. Through the trees, he saw the wagon, then stumbled and fell.

He clawed for the sack and rifle, grabbed them, then stood up, momentarily losing his bearings. As he turned around, he saw his assailant had managed his feet and was staggering toward him.

"Wait," Moses yelled to the wagon, then bolted downhill.

He emerged from the woods, just ahead of the wagon. He waved the rifle wildly over his head. "Stop, stop," he yelled.

He saw the driver make a move for his gun, then realized the guard stopped him from pulling it.

The driver braked the wagon as Moses approached, gasping for breath. "Hope . . . you folks've . . . got room for a . . . passenger," he panted, as he looked from the driver to the guard. His mouth opened wider in surprise. The guard was a woman and not just any woman but the woman he had saved the night before.

"Why, Missy, you're okay?"

She nodded. "I never got a chance to say thank you."

"Giving me a ride will be plenty of thanks enough," he replied.

"Come on," she said, scooting closer to Blake.

As Moses climbed in the driver's box, he saw his unarmed assailant standing by a tree not thirty yards away. "Let's get out of here," Moses yelled. "Pronto."

11

Penny Heath studied Moses Baldwin as he dropped a flour sack and gun belt on the floorboard, then squeezed his big hands around his rifle. She remembered his hulking figure from her encounter with Buford.

"You didn't stay around for introductions so I never knew if he hurt you?"

"Not as bad as he was going to."

"I'm glad to hear that, yes I am."

Blake Corley leaned forward and stared at the black man. "You're Moses Baldwin, aren't you?"

Moses nodded. "How'd you know?"

"The sheriff wanted to talk to you."

Moses gulped. "About what?"

Penny answered. "Buford's beating."

"Is that all?"

"Is there more?" Blake asked.

Moses sighed. "I can't say for certain, no sir."

"It wouldn't have anything to do with those gunshots we heard before you came charging down the mountain, would it?" Blake stared past Penny at Moses.

"No offense, sir," Moses said, pointing down the road, "but I'd feel a mite safer if you'd watch where you're going, unless you want to wind up in the river."

Blake jerked the lines and the mule team eased away from the road's edge. "What about the gunshots?"

"Some fellow up there was trying to kill some meat."

"Wouldn't have been dark meat, would it?"

"You two quit badgering each other," Penny interjected. "I don't care what either of you did. Both of you helped me out of a tight spot." She turned to Baldwin. "I'm Penny Heath."

He took off his hat and nodded. "Pleased to make your acquaintance, ma'am. I'll just keep to calling you, Missy, if you don't mind. Some white men don't take kindly to a black man calling a white woman by her name. Who's your friend?"

"I'm Blake Corley."

"Oh, the one that bought the Haney claim."

Blake felt his cheeks heating up. He jiggled the reins. "And you're the one everybody calls Black Baldy?"

Moses spit over the side of the wagon. "My friends don't."

Penny cleared her throat. "If we're gonna make it to Durango, we can't be at each other's throats all the way."

Moses nodded.

Blake pursed his lips. "Only way we'll stay from each other's throats is if we come clean about everything." Blake glanced at Baldwin. "So there's no secrets between us, no suspicions. You agree to that Moses Baldwin?"

Moses cast Blake a hard stare, then bit his lip as he nodded. "You go ahead." The black man grinned.

Blake shook his head. "You start off."

Penny screamed in exasperation. "You two. I'll start. I'm a prostitute or was. I'm carrying a child."

Both men hung their heads, neither looking at her as she spoke.

"Belle Farthing, the woman that ran the house where I worked, wanted me to drop the child. I couldn't do that, even if I don't know who its father is. I ran away, not getting any of the money I was due. Belle sent her man to beat me so I'd lose the child. Moses saved me from that beating. By taking me out of Silverton, Blake saved me from the beatings to come. He didn't want to take me, but I offered to warm his bed."

Moses grumbled.

"Don't think poorly of him, Moses. He refused the offer, but agreed to take me anyway." Penny reached to pat Blake on the arm. "Go ahead."

Blake looked from Penny to Moses, then back at the road. "I was a Kansas sodbuster and the fool who bought the Haney claim. I thought I could get rich. I never saw sign of anything and I knew I'd go crazy if I stayed the winter. I missed the last stage before the snows set in, but I was desperate to get out and the freight agent agreed to let me drive this wagon back to Durango if I'd take the bodies of the driver and the guard killed in the robbery."

Moses looked at Blake. "This wagon's got bodies in it and that's it?"

Blake nodded. "Nothing else, save a few supplies. You scared?"

"I reckon not. I was in Alabama during the War of the Rebellion. I saw plenty of bodies and buried quite a few. I even figured on becoming an undertaker after I got my freedom, but blacks didn't have the money to pay for a funeral and whites didn't want me touching their dead. So I came out west, figuring if I couldn't dig graves I could dig gold or silver. Take something out of the ground rather than put it back in."

Blake cleared his throat. "Then why aren't you back in Silverton digging? It wouldn't have anything to do with those gunshots, would it?"

Moses turned his dark eyes full bore toward Blake.

Blake knew Moses was assessing him, trying to decide if he could be trusted. How Moses responded would determine if Blake could trust *him*.

"I learned to avoid trouble," Moses started. "It's the best

way for a black man to survive. I bought my supplies in white stores just before closing time. I took my drinks in the backs of saloons rather than out front with the others. Last night I went to town for supplies and a drink. I'm in the back of the saloon when Missy ran by, this brute chasing her out back. It didn't seem like a fair race or a fair fight to me. I caught him and taught him a few manners, which wasn't a smart thing for a black man to do to a white man. No matter that it wasn't right for him to be hurting Missy.

"It's late when I started back up river for my cabin. I'm passing through the woods when I seen three men hiding a couple bodies. They come running and shooting at me. They recognize me because I hear one of them call me Black Baldy. I skedaddle it back to town, hide out in a woodshed. I figure the three killers'll either kill me or blame me for killing those two poor fellows they was burying. Who's the sheriff gonna believe? A darkie or three white men? I had to get out of town."

Blake figured Moses could be trusted. "Sheriff didn't say anything about you being wanted for murder. He's just interested in talking to you about Buford's beating. What about the gunshots?"

"After I saw the freight agent harnessing a team, I figured he was sending a wagon to Durango. I slipped out of town and hid on the mountain until you approached. A man was waiting there with a rifle and pistol and started shooting at me. I outwitted him and took his guns."

"Was it one of the three men that tried to get you last night?" Blake asked.

Moses shrugged. "I can't be certain. I didn't get a good look at any of them, though one seemed to have a red beard and another looked to be wearing an eye patch."

Blake looked at Penny. He could tell what she was thinking. One of the men Blake had seen around the stove in the freight office wore an eye patch.

"It wasn't either of them," Moses said, "but maybe it was the third one."

"Did you kill him?" Blake asked.

Moses shook his head. "I thought I knocked him out, but as I was climbing in the wagon, I saw him staring at us."

"What's it all mean?" Penny asked.

Blake shrugged. "I'm not certain, other than we need to get to Durango as fast as we can because we don't know who'll be following us from Silverton."

Moses twisted around and looked back up the road. "It's not just men that may be following us." He pointed to the mountaintops.

Penny turned about and Blake glanced over his shoulder for a moment. He saw a bank of gray clouds creeping over the mountains.

"Them's snow clouds for sure," Moses announced.

Penny shivered.

"We'd best get as far as we can before dark," Blake said. "No telling how much snow we'll have to pull through tomorrow."

"I can spell you on the reins, if you need it," Moses offered.

They rode until it was too dark to see. Blake drew up the wagon on the road for there was no place else to turn. To one side roared the Animas River, oblivious to the cold and the snow. To the other side was a steep slope. Blake set the brake and jumped from the wagon. Moses helped Penny down onto the road. In the darkness the snow, glazed over with ice, crunched with their every step.

"At least no one will be able to slip up on us," Blake said.

Despite the darkness, Penny insisted on making her way down to the river to wash the blood from her cut leg. Blake protested, but she went anyway, finding narrow footholds down the five-foot ledge that separated the road from the river.

Moses scurried up the mountain slope, gathering what wood he could find while Blake searched for rocks that he could wedge beneath the wagon wheels as extra security that the mules wouldn't run away with the wagon. Blake chose to leave the mules harnessed because there was no place to tie them and nothing for them to graze on. He cursed Alfred Donner for not loading some sacks of grain to feed the team.

By the time Penny returned, Moses had built a fire behind a boulder to screen it from the icy winds that picked up through the gorge. Penny backed up to the fire and lifted her skirt to feel the full warmth on her calf. Blake studied her white calf, then turned away embarrassed when she caught him looking.

"Other men have seen more." She smiled.

Moses sat with his back to the fire, not looking at Penny. Instead, he dug into his flour sack and pulled out a partial loaf of bread, split it in thirds and shared it with Penny and Blake.

"There's blankets and a couple buffalo robes under the tarp," Blake said. "Where you figure we ought to sleep, Mose?"

The black man finished a bite of bread. "It smells like snow blowing in. Missy can sleep in the back, under the tarp. You and I can sleep under the wagon."

"I don't know," Penny said, looking nervously at the wagon.

"Missy, if anybody grabs you, it won't be those two."

Blake laughed until Penny scowled at him.

"Another thing," Blake said, turning to the black man. "We better split turns standing watch."

Moses nodded. "I don't want anything but the snow sneaking up on us tonight and I don't really want that."

12

Darkness and the snowfall had set in by the time Bibb Clack stumbled back to Silverton and pounded on the rear door of the freight office. He was still dazed from the knot on his head and further numbed by the biting cold that cut right through his clothes like a knife. He slammed his fist repeatedly against the door before it opened. Clack shoved his way past Alfred Donner and marched straight for the large stove out front.

After barring the back door, Donner lit a lamp and trailed after him. "Did you get him?" Donner caught up with Clack, grabbed him by the arm and spun him around. Donner saw the bruise and knot across Clack's temple. "By damn, he got you, didn't he?"

Holding his hands out to the stove, Clack nodded. "He jumped me, took my rifle and gun belt."

"You see where he went?"

Clack nodded. "Down the Durango road."

Donner scratched his whiskered chin. "That might not be bad, if we scared him away." Donner grinned. "In fact, that might be damn good. What was he riding?"

"He was walking."

Clapping his hands together, Donner laughed. "You boys must've really put the scare in him last night, to walk away from Silverton in this kind of weather."

Shrugging, Clack turned around to let the fire warm his back. "He walked to the road and caught the freight wagon."

Donner cursed. "The freight wagon?"

"Yeah, what difference does it make?"

"What difference does it make?" Donner screamed. "Maybe a hundred thousand dollars difference for us."

"Huh?"

"Don't you understand. The darkie saw the three of you hiding two bodies, bodies that are supposed to be in the coffins. If he makes the connection, he'll ride away from Durango a rich man."

"He's too dumb to think that through."

"He wasn't too dumb to give you the slip, now was he, Bibb?"

"Hell, Alf, it was your damn idea to send the money out in the coffins anyway. If I'd had my druthers, I'd just as soon be spending the money now."

Donner scoffed. "Instead of money, you'd be spending time in Sheriff Johnson's jail right now, if you'd had your way. Stew'd know who stole the money."

Clack turned to face the stove, thinking of little more than the warmth his body craved.

Frustrated, Donner strode away. He placed the lamp on the freight counter, then kicked at the floor.

"Hell," Clack added, "they'll probably freeze to death and somebody else'll find them after the spring thaw. Hell, you've outsmarted yourself and us out of a hundred thousand dollars, you bastard."

Donner spun around. "We've got to go after it."

"You ain't been outside, Alf. It's like ice out there."

"We'll ride to get Luther and Dick, then take out after them in the morning."

"We don't have horses, Alf."

"There's a team of mules in the stable. We can ride them."

"We don't have enough saddles."

"Some of us can ride bareback. You're going, Bibb, or you'll forfeit your share of the loot."

Clack doubled his fists and stepped toward Donner. "You're not taking what's mine."

"If you don't go along, won't any of it be yours."

"You bastard, you didn't go along with me and Dick and Luther when we killed Barney and Pug."

Donner couldn't argue with that. Instead, he strode around the freight counter, bent down and picked up the shotgun Pug had carried on his final ride. He lifted it over the counter, cocked the hammers, and pointed it square at Clack's gut.

Clack paled.

"You better pay attention to what I have to say, Bibb, or I'll blow you to pieces. We'll do things my way or we won't do them at all. If you'd killed Black Baldy like you should have, we wouldn't be disputing things."

Clack nodded.

"You're either with me, Bibb, or you're against me. And if you're against me, you won't be against me long." The shotgun was as steady and menacing as Donner's glare.

Clack melted like snow before a fire. "Whatever you say, Alf."

Donner nodded and released the twin hammers on the shotgun. "That's more like it. You stay by the stove and warm up while I get our mounts. Then we'll ride out and find Luther, then head to the darkie's cabin, stay the night there, then get on the trail early in the morning."

Turning back to the stove, Clack said nothing.

Donner dressed, then grabbed his gun belt from a peg on the back wall and buckled it around his waist. He hurriedly wrestled his coat on, then snatched his hat from a peg and tugged it down over his head.

The snow was picking up as Donner raced to the stable. He

unlatched the door and slid inside, then lit a lamp. The mules were jittery, tossing their heads and stamping their feet. He managed to come up with four bridles and three saddles, leaving him one short. As he saddled the mules, he doubted more and more that his plan could succeed. He had no doubt he would find the freight wagon and the money, but if he abandoned the freight office, Sheriff Johnson would grow suspicious and perhaps link the disappearance with the murder of Barney and Pug.

To make matters worse, Bibb Clack had started asking too many questions instead of following orders. That was unhealthy to Donner's plans, damn unhealthy. Anyway, Clack was the dumbest and weakest of Donner's three confederates. As he saddled the last mule, Donner figured out how to avoid the sheriff's suspicions and remove Clack as a problem.

Donner rigged a fourth mule as a pack animal, then retreated back inside the freight office. Clack's eyes widened in fear as Donner burst into the front room. Bending behind the counter, Donner picked up four empty canvas bags. When he stood up, he saw Clack cowering behind the stove.

"What'd you think, Bibb, I was reaching for the shotgun again."

Clack nodded.

Donner laughed and tossed a couple bags which landed by the stove. "Fill those with grub from my room. We'll need something to eat until we can claim our money. I'll fetch a couple blankets and the last of our buffalo robes. That should get us by."

Warily, Clack retreated to the back room while Donner grabbed what boxes of ammunition he had from under the freight counter. He dumped them in the canvas sack, then shoved the sawed-off shotgun inside as well. That done, he retreated to the back room and saw Clack eyeing him over his shoulder. Donner packed two blankets atop the shotgun and ammunition, then tied the canvas straps on the bag. Next, he shoved three more blankets in the second canvas bag and closed it. He placed both bags by the door as Clack approached with the other two.

"You filled those with food?" he asked.

"All you had."

"What about a gun for me?" Clack asked.

Studying Clack for a moment, Donner nodded, and patted the pistol at his side. "You can use mine, if need be or the shotgun I packed in one of the bags. Just give me a hand and get this stuff out to the stable."

Donner followed Clack outside into the cold hard wind. The blowing snow and ice stung their faces like tiny insects. Donner tossed his canvas bags into the stable, taking the two that Clack carried, then sending him back into the freight station for fear he might see that only three animals were saddled.

"Visit the stove and stay as warm as you can, Bibb."

As Clack retreated to the freight office, Donner hurriedly loaded the pack mule and tied the canvas bags down. Then, he strung the mules' reins together and led the animals out behind the stable, tying them to a post.

Then he retreated inside to find Clack by the stove.

"You ready?"

Shrugging, Clack stepped toward the counter. "I'll kill the lamp."

"Nope, don't want people to think we're not here, Bibb."

Clack stepped around the counter and marched into the back room, lingering by Donner's bed.

Donner laughed as he stopped within reach of Clack. "Bibb, you want my gun since you lost yours?"

"Sure."

Slowly, Donner drew back his coat, pulled the gun from the holster, then shoved the revolver in Clack's gut. Clack's heavy coat muffled the explosion. Clack screamed, then fell back onto the bed, mumbling and gurgling. Donner leaned over him and pressed the gun to his heart. He fired again. Clack twitched, then fell still.

Donner reholstered his pistol and lifted Clack's legs up on the bed, straightening him out to make it look like he had been sleeping. Then Donner retreated to the corner for a tin of coal oil. He doused Clack's body, soaked a trail all the way from the bed to the stove, then tossed the empty can aside. From beneath the counter he grabbed another coal oil tin, this one half full, and soaked the floor. Retreating to the back room, he tossed the other tin aside and reached in his pocket for matches.

At the back door, he nodded at Clack. "Maybe this'll keep you warm."

He scratched the match against the wall, then flung it toward Clack. The body exploded in flame and a trail of fire swooshed out the door into the front room.

Donner raced outside and around the stable, untied the lead mule, mounted and rode at a trot away from the freight station as the snow swirled in the wind, keeping people off the streets and inside. The empty streets would give the fire time to take a solid hold before being discovered. Even though the snow made it difficult to see, the glow through the haze left no doubt that something was ablaze.

From somewhere Donner finally heard the alarm being raised. "Fire," came one voice, then another.

Moments later he heard the clang of the fire bell. The whole town would be turning out to save the freight office and him, but they would be too late. Come morning, when the embers had cooled, Sheriff Stewart Johnson would find a body in Donner's bed and assume it was the station agent.

Bibb Clack should have never turned surly. Donner laughed. With poor Bibb's demise, Donner would be due a bigger share of the loot.

13

Alfred Donner reached the trees beyond Silverton and turned his mount into the woods, the other mules tramping behind Donner's, their hooves crunching through the glazed snow. Donner glanced over his shoulder and could just make out a glow in the snowfall. The freight office was surely ablaze for Donner to see even a glow through the wind's fury.

Donner pointed the animals toward the spot where Dick Pincham had told him he would find the shallow graves of Barney and Pug. As he neared the place, he shouted, "Luther, Luther Perry? Where are you?"

He rode a hundred yards and all that answered him was the crunch of the snow and the whistle of the wind through the trees.

"Luther, Luther Perry?"

"Is that you, Alf?" came a hoarse call.

Donner recognized Luther's voice and answered, "Yeah."

"It's about time you showed up. I'm so cold and stiff it'll take me a week to warm up."

Donner saw a dark form emerge from behind a brush shelter made in the vee of two fallen trees.

Luther staggered forward, a thick buffalo robe wrapped around his shoulders. "Did one of the boys get Black Baldy?"

"Nope. Fact is, the darkie got Bibb."

"Now we'll kill him for sure."

"But Bibb never gave up. Even though he was shot, he walked to the freight office and told me Black Baldy had hitched a ride with Corley in the freight wagon. You know what that means, don't you?"

"Both of them'll freeze instead of just Corley."

Donner shook his head as he untied the string of mules behind him. He tossed the reins. "We're going after them, Luther. We've got to get the money."

Shivering, Perry stepped to the mule and grabbed the line. "You weren't worried about Corley taking the money. How come now?"

"Corley didn't see the three of you hiding the bodies. There's the chance they'll realize the coffins have the strongboxes instead of the bodies. If they do, they'll skip Colorado with the money and we'll be as poor as ever."

"Damn them," Perry said, shoving his foot in the stirrup and swinging atop the mule.

Donner nudged his mule. "Did anybody come near the graves?"

"I never saw a soul. I chased away a couple of wolves, but you're the first person I've seen since I've been up here."

They rode in silence, gradually swinging toward the river and following it to Moses Baldwin's cabin. The snow made it hard to see and Donner was surprised to finally spot the yellow glow of a lamp not thirty yards ahead. He squinted and could just make out the darker outline of the cabin. Had Bibb Clack been wrong? Had Moses Baldwin returned to his cabin?

Donner started to draw his gun, then suddenly understood. No wonder Dick Pincham had volunteered to guard the cabin. The son of a bitch had set himself up inside and waited in the warmth of Baldwin's own cabin for his return.

Donner cupped his hands over his mouth. "Dick Pincham," he yelled. "This is Alf and Luther riding in."

"The bastard," cried Perry. "I'm sitting out in the cold and he's staying in a warm cabin and looking out the window. Damn him."

"Dick Pincham," Donner shouted. "We're riding in." He touched his mule's flank and the animal advanced. Slowly the cabin appeared out of the snowfall.

The square of light was joined by a lit rectangle as Pincham opened the door. "Well, ride on in before you wake up the dead." Pincham's words and laugh were muffled by the snow.

Quickly, Donner and Perry jumped from their mules, tied them to a hitching post, then darted in. Pincham closed the door.

The cabin was little more than a narrow bed, plank table, stool, crate of food, a lamp, and a small stove, but it was shelter and it was warm. Donner and Perry stamped their feet and slapped their coats as they edged toward the stove.

"What brings you fellows out?" Pincham grinned. "You're the first visitors I've had since I moved in. How was it watching the graves, Luther?" Pincham fell down on the bed, laughing.

"We've got problems," Donner started. "Bibb's dead. Baldwin got him leaving town, but Bibb made it back to the freight office and told me Baldwin'd hitched up with Corley in the freight wagon."

"Guess that changes things," Pincham said. "Damn! I'll have to give up my warm cabin here and catch them before they realize they're not carrying bodies."

Holding his palms to the stove, Donner nodded. "That's about the size of it."

"Hell, Dick, you ain't got nothing to complain about. I spent the night outside in the cold."

"Luther, I thought about you while I was feeding my fire." Perry growled.

"We'll ride out a couple hours before sunrise. Make sure nobody spots us when we pass town," Donner announced.

"Hell, Alf, everyone'll know you're gone when the freight office doesn't open up."

Donner pondered whether to reveal the fate of the freight station, then decided it would do no harm. "There ain't no more freight office in Silverton."

Pincham and Perry jerked their heads around and stared hard.

"What do you mean, Alf?" Pincham asked.

"It burned down tonight."

"Well, hell, Alf, that'll just make the sheriff suspicious. The place burns down and you're nowhere around to be found."

Donner laughed. "Oh, they'll find me."

"What do mean?" The bewildered Perry shrugged.

Pincham's eyes narrowed and he bit his lip. "They'll find you dead, is that it, Alf?"

Donner nodded.

Perry threw up his arms. "What are you talking about?"

"I died in my sleep, Luther."

Perry took off his hat and flung it on the bed. "What is going on? You ain't dead." Perry rubbed his red beard, trying to make sense out of it all.

Pincham leaned back against the wall and laughed. "Poor Bibb, roasted before he ever got to hell."

Perry squinted his eyes. "What about Bibb?"

"Hell, Luther, do we have to explain everything to you?"

"I guess the hell you do, Dick."

Shaking his head, Pincham grinned. "After Bibb died, Alf put him in his bed."

"Why?"

"Then set fire to the building."

Luther scratched his head. "But why?"

"So folks will think Alf died in the fire. Damn smart thinking, Alf."

Donner nodded. "I was pleased with the notion."

Perry pointed his finger at Donner. "You burned up Bibb?"

"Now you've got it, Luther. I'm proud of you," Pincham taunted.

"That was a damn rotten thing to do to Bibb, Alf. A man deserves a decent burial."

Donner scoffed. "You didn't think that about Barney and Pug. Besides, Luther, Bibb's death will mean a bigger share for you."

Perry turned away, shaking his head. "It still don't seem right, no sir, it sure don't."

14

Morning seeped past the bitter cold on the mountain road. The snow had stopped but not before eighteen inches had piled up. The morning light was diffused by the blanket of gray clouds that lingered overhead, threatening to drop more snow.

Having taken the first watch, Blake Corley was ensconced in a buffalo robe beneath the wagon. His fingers were stiff with cold and his ears and cheeks were numb from the frigid air. Blake opened his eyelids slowly, as if they might be frozen shut. He glanced to his side to look out across the road, but all he saw was a ledge of white. The snow had drifted around the wagon until it had virtually boxed him in. Blake flung back the buffalo robe and blanket, then clawed his way through the bank of snow.

Though heavy with moisture, the snow was easily shoveled aside and Blake emerged into a world that was covered with snow. The trees, the rocks, the road, all were powdered with white. The canvas cover over the wagon bed was heaped with a foot-and-a-half of snow. Blake swatted at the snow on the lid of the side-mounted toolbox, then opened it up and removed the shovel. With the shovel, he began to scrape the snow off the canvas.

"What's that?" cried Penny Heath from beneath the canvas where she had slept.

"It's just me," Blake replied, "clearing the snow."

Shortly, the open corner of the canvas tarp flew back and Penny poked her head up like a gopher coming out of its hole. "Brrr."

Blake worked his way around the wagon, knocking snow off the canvas, then the seat. "You get any sleep?"

"Mostly, I got cold."

"Me, too." Blake circled the team, then returned the shovel to the toolbox. Squatting, he poked his arm under the wagon, fished around a moment, then pulled the blanket and buffalo robe out. As he stood, he shook them free of the clinging snow, then handed both to Penny. She stored them under the canvas.

Blake plowed back through the snow to the mules. Their gray and brown coats were matted with snow and their nostrils ringed with ice flakes where their breath vapors had condensed and frozen. Their lifeless dark eyes were circled with snow. The mules stood motionless, barely moving as Blake walked by, slapping at their hides to knock off some of the snow.

As Blake retreated to Penny, he saw Moses Baldwin trudging down the road toward him. The black man was wrapped in a snow-matted buffalo robe, his hat powdered with snow and his face splotched white in places. "You look like a ghost, Mose."

"It's as close as I'll ever come to looking like a white man."

"Unless we get more snow," Blake answered.

"I'm cold and hungry," Moses said, "but I figure we ought to start moving. Time spent building a fire and fixing breakfast is time lost. Not that I've got anything against food and heat right now, just I figure those boys'll be on our tail."

Blake turned to Penny. "Think you can get by without a warm breakfast."

She nodded. "Time's a wasting."

"There's food in my sack we can eat on the road."

As Moses neared the wagon, Penny motioned for him to

approach. She brushed the snow away from his coat and cheeks.

"Thank you, Missy. You want to ride up front or stay back here with you buddies."

"They were perfect gentlemen," she said, "but I'll ride up front."

Grinning, Moses laid his rifle down on the canvas cover and held his arms out to her. "The snow's a little deep, I'll give you a lift."

Penny wriggled out through the canvas opening and stood in the wagon bed. Moses slid an arm around her shoulder, then another under her knees and carried her to the wagon seat. Before he sat her down, he laughed. "Guess if I was going to keep you dry, I should've shoveled the driver's box."

Penny reached out and brushed the powder from the seat, then began scooping snow from the driver's box. "Am I getting heavy?"

"Missy, I'm a miner. I've toted rocks that are twice as heavy and not nearly as pretty."

Penny giggled. "That'll do."

Moses stood her up in the wagon box and she finished clearing the seat and emptying the floorboard of snow.

As Moses retreated for his rifle, Blake moved around the wagon, prying from beneath each wheel the rocks he had wedged there.

Moses retied the canvas tarp, then grabbed his rifle and trudged around to the front just as Blake climbed in beside Penny. Moses removed the buffalo robe from his shoulders and handed it to Penny. "Wrap in this, Missy, it'll keep you a little warmer." She took the hide and threw it around herself.

The wagon shook as Moses climbed up beside her. "If we don't get those mules moving, they'll turn to icicles."

"I was waiting on you, Mose," Blake untied the stiff reins, then released the brake lever and shook the lines. The mules were sluggish to react, but gradually they leaned into the harnesses and started down the road to Durango.

Moses leaned forward and picked up his flour sack, heavy with the gun belt and revolver he had taken from his attacker the day before. "I've got some tins of peaches, if you want some eats. I figure they're plenty cold." Receiving no answer from Penny or Blake, Moses shook his head. "What's a matter, you 'fraid of my cooking?"

Blake grinned. "We got to get through the tin to get to the peaches."

"Now, now," Moses said, reaching inside his coat to the new hunting knife strapped behind his waist. He pulled out the knife and waved it in the air. "This'll cut just about anything." He poked the knife in the top of the tin and worked it around the perimeter. When the lid came free he tossed it on the trail, then pried a sliver of frozen peach and syrup from the can and offered it on the knife tip to Missy. She took it and gave it to Blake, then took the next sliver for herself. Moses ate a bite, then divvied out bites one at a time until the can was empty.

Travel was slow at first, but the mules gradually warmed up and grew accustomed to the footing. Though the road was treacherous, the load in the wagon was light and the mules held their strength.

Moses kept glancing over his back, watching the road behind them, looking for sign of anyone who might be following them. "How are we heeled for battle?" he asked.

Blake shrugged. "The only thing I figured to be fighting was the weather. I've got my revolver and fifteen or twenty cartridges in my gun belt."

"I hope you're a damn good shot, then."

Moses slapped his coat pocket. "I got the pistol I took from that Buford fellow and the rifle, pistol, and gun belt I took from the fellow that started shooting at me before I made your acquaintance. They're both forty-fives. What about yours, Blake?"

"It's a forty-five."

"Good." Moses toed at the flour sack at his feet. "I got a

fifty-count box of forty-five ammunition so I figure we've about a hundred or so cartridges."

Penny shoved her gloved hand into her coat pocket. "I've got this." She pulled out her two-shot Derringer.

"Missy, why didn't you tell us you was carrying a cannon. You fire that thing off and it's likely to start the damnedest avalanche you've ever seen."

Meekly, she shoved the Derringer back in her coat.

"It could come in handy," Blake admitted.

Moses nodded. "Just let me know before you shoot it so I can cover my ears." He grinned, his teeth shining as bright as the snow, until he realized he had hurt her feelings. "Missy, I was just funning you."

She smiled.

"They'll have to be awfully close for that to do you any good," Blake said.

"In my line of work, you got plenty close."

Blake felt his cheeks heat with embarrassment and he shook the reins.

Moses just laughed. "That peashooter must be what kept your two buddies in the back from pawing at you last night."

Penny cocked her head toward Moses and grinned. "Remember I'm close enough for my peashooter to put a hole in you."

Moses laughed harder.

Blake figured they made about six miles by noon. They stopped only once, to stretch their legs and shake out a little of the stiffness, then climbed back in the wagon and continued toward Durango.

By midafternoon they approached a narrow granite canyon. The road clung to the steep mountain wall on one side. The other side was a jagged precipice that dropped fifty feet to the roaring water below. Blake drew up on the reins, dragging the wagon to a halt and studied the narrow canyon. There was little room for error.

"The going'll be slow for a while," Blake said, letting out a deep breath.

Moses stood in the floorboard and stretched his massive arms. He turned around, then froze. He squinted to make sure his eyes weren't playing tricks on him. "We've got company," he announced.

Blake and Penny spun around.

Moses pointed to a spot maybe a mile behind them. "Three or four men, looks like to me."

"Damn," Blake said, "just as we're getting to the worst part of the road."

"You think it's them?" Penny asked.

"Who else would be out in this weather?" Blake answered. "Missy, hold the fire on that cannon."

Blake settled back in his seat and took firm hold on the reins. "We better start moving."

"Let's just don't move too fast, Blake. I don't like the idea of them catching up with us, but I don't like the thought of falling over that cliff."

When Moses and Penny sat down, Blake eased the mules ahead down the treacherous road.

"They can catch up with us over this stretch of road," Moses said, "but I figure they'll wait until dark to attack."

"That'll give us a little time to think up something," Blake said.

Moses looked toward the ledge, then shook his head. "Do either of you two know how to fly?"

Sheriff Stewart Johnson toed through the rubble of the Animas Freight and Stage Station. Little remained except burnt sections of wall, timbers that had caved in when the building collapsed, and wooden shingles that had survived after absorbing moisture from the snow. A few shards of black and charred wood poked through the snow, and in places glowing embers hissed and sent up steam through holes in the snow. But mostly, the remains of the freight station were covered beneath a blanket of snow.

The dim early morning light made the search more difficult, but Johnson wanted to inspect the station before the curious arose and started rummaging through the debris. The overnight snow didn't help, Silverton taking up to two additional feet. It was going to be a long, cold winter. Johnson shivered at the thought, then moved to the rear of the building where Alfred Donner bunked.

Johnson hadn't seen Donner since the fire. Nobody had. Johnson suspected Donner was dead beneath the rubble, but something didn't seem right about the fire. Bad luck was a part of mining camp life, but the Animas Freight and Stage Company had suffered more than its share, even for a mining camp. Two of the company's men had been killed. Payrolls totaling a hundred thousand dollars had been stolen on a disguised money run that few people would have known about. Now, the freight office itself had burned down.

In addition to Donner, where were Dick Pincham, Luther Perry, and Bibb Clack? They were sometime freight line employees, sometime vagrants who hung around the freight office as long as Donner would tolerate them. They weren't the type of men Johnson would have trusted in any position, but trustworthy men could be as hard to find as virtuous women in a mining camp.

Johnson bent, grabbed a section of charred wall, and wrestled it from the debris, tossed it aside, then kicked at some burnt shards of wood. He waded deeper into the rubble, being careful to avoid any nails that could poke through the sole of his boot and puncture his foot. He slipped his foot under a piece of wood to kick it aside and his boot snagged on a piece of wire. He tugged the wire back with his foot, then nodded. It was a coil of wire. He had found what he was after, the bedspring. He worked his foot out of the coil and the wire fell limply among the debris.

Bending over the clump of debris, he began to lift charred and brittle lumber, then tossed it aside, cratering the snow where it fell. Some of the wood disintegrated in his glove. He scraped away debris and snow, gradually working his way down to the blackened clumps of the cotton mattress and the bedspring.

Exploring the remains of the bed with his hand, his glove wrapped around something that was neither wood, nor debris. He gritted his teeth and lifted the object. It was a man's arm, burnt almost beyond recognition except for the nubs where fingers had been. Johnson released the arm and shook his head. Maybe he had been wrong about Alfred Donner.

Johnson backed away from the body, looking around to be sure no one watched, then retreated down the street to the undertaker. Johnson's stomach felt squeamish as it always did when he found a body. Death was something a sane man never got accustomed to until his own, Johnson guessed. Then, it was only out of necessity. Johnson couldn't understand how an undertaker could stomach his job. Of course, a lot of men had the same questions about a lawman's work. Some horses were meant to ride, some to pull a plow, and some to run free, Johnson decided.

At the undertaker's home—a modest house with a fresh coat of whitewash on it—Johnson knocked on the door and waited what seemed like forever for him to answer.

The undertaker, dressed in a nightshirt and woolen socks, opened the door, rubbing his eyes. "Find a body in the fire?"

Johnson nodded.

"Can't it wait until later?"

"It could wait to the spring thaw, if I weren't an impatient sort, but I am. I don't want a circus when we remove the body."

The undertaker shrugged. "Maybe you should charge admission." The undertaker started shutting the door. "I'll meet you there."

"Be quick."

Grumbling, the undertaker closed the door.

Johnson circled back to the freight office and found a couple curious men poking through the rubble while they waited for the eatery across the street to open.

"If you fellows are volunteer firemen, you're too late. If you're not, be about your business."

The two men skulked across the street to wait.

Johnson strode past the debris to the stables that were scorched on the side facing the fire, but otherwise undamaged. He opened the door and walked inside, noting the two mules tied in their stalls. The animals' legs were cut and streaked with frozen blood. In their panic to get away from the fire, the mules had tried to kick their way out of the barn. They were still skittish, jerking at their ropes and twitching their rear legs.

Johnson retreated back outside and as he was shutting the

stable door, he froze. He poked his head back inside, finding it odd there were but two mules. Generally the freight company kept six on hand during winter, enough to pull a freight wagon through the snow, if need be. Johnson confirmed there were but two mules. The freight wagon that was robbed had come in with six mules and left with six. There should still be six in the stable. It was possible someone had stolen the other four. Johnson could understand mules being stolen if spring were approaching, but this was the start of winter. Mules would be nothing but a burden, needing feed, water, and shelter. The missing mules stumped him. He closed and latched the stable, then retreated to the rubble. He waited another ten minutes before he saw the undertaker driving the hearse toward him.

The sheriff motioned for the undertaker to bring the hearse around back. The undertaker guided the hearse to the rear of the rubble, then jumped down and scurried to remove a wooden coffin. Johnson helped him carry the coffin into the debris.

The men across the street started shouting they'd found a body and shortly a couple dozen men stood watching Johnson and the undertaker. Johnson gave them a hard glare, but they were fascinated by the spectacle of death and didn't budge.

"Terrible way to die, a fire," the undertaker said as he eased toward burnt bed. He cleared away more debris and gradually exposed the full body. "Do you know if Alf has any relatives? I can put him up until spring, if need be. If he's like Pug and Barney, they didn't have any kin to speak of. At least not this side of the Mississippi River."

Johnson shrugged. "Don't know." He looked at the black-ened body, shriveled and contorted, then shook his head. "You're right, a terrible way to die."

The undertaker leaned to grab the body by the shoulders. "You get his legs."

Grimacing, Johnson moved toward the feet as the under-taker gripped his shoulder. Johnson was glad to be wearing gloves as he grabbed each leg. Together the two lifted the body and eased it toward the coffin. Johnson was surprised by its lightness. As he fit it in the coffin, he was also surprised to realize that Donner had been wearing his boots when he died. For a man sleeping outside, that would have been one thing, but not for a man in the warmth of a building. Johnson released the body and stood staring at the boots until the undertaker covered the coffin.

As the undertaker drove away, Johnson scratched his head. Maybe he was thinking too much. No doubt he had been trying to figure out who had robbed the freight wagon and who killed Barney and Pug, but this seemed so strange. He shrugged and walked back to his office in the courthouse. He had a cup of coffee for breakfast then when stores and saloons began to open he went up and down the street asking proprietors if anyone was spending more money than normal.

Right before noon he heard someone running down the street, yelling, "Sheriff, sheriff."

Johnson stepped out of the mercantile into the cold.

"There you are," said a breathless man, a hunting rifle in his hands. "I found a couple bodies in the trees up yonder." He pointed toward a wooded hill. "Two men. I was hunting game, hoping to get some venison, and ran upon some wolves fighting over a kill. When I got close enough. I seen it was two men. I shot two of the wolves but the others'll be back."

"You got a horse?"

"No."

"Come with me. We'll ride double."

Johnson ran to the nearby livery where he kept his bay. He told the stable hand to saddle the animal as quickly as he could, then asked the hunter for more details.

When the stable hand returned with his horse, Johnson climbed in the saddle, then helped the hunter on behind him. They trotted down the street, then turned toward the woods, Johnson following the hunter's directions.

In twenty minutes the men were riding on the tree-studded

hill and the hunter pointed out the spot. Johnson saw the carcasses of two dead wolves and a lump of snow.

"Where are the dead men?"

"They're in a shallow grave," the hunter answered. "The wolves must have dug them up."

Johnson drew up short of the bodies, helped the hunter to the ground, then handed him the reins as he dismounted. "You stay here."

Out of instinct, he drew his pistol. He trudged toward the bodies, thinking what a bad week it had been around Silverton. He toed the dead wolves, disgusted at the flesh and cloth caught in the jaws of one.

He walked to the other side of the mound and looked in the shallow hole. It was men all right. He saw a hand with clumps of dirt on it and the side of a man's head peeking from among the snow and ground. He squatted over the grave and grabbed the dead man's head. For a moment, it didn't budge as he tried to twist it around to see his face. Then it gave and twisted toward Johnson.

Johnson fell back in horror. "What the hell?" he cried.

It was Barney.

He shoved his pistol in his holster and began to claw at the second body, quickly confirming what he then suspected. The second body was Pug. But these two men were supposed to be on the way to their kin in Durango. That's what Donner had said, but the undertaker said Barney and Pug had no kin west of the Mississippi.

If Barney and Pug weren't in the coffins going to Durango, then who was? Or, what was?

"The payroll," Johnson said. "That's it."

The payroll was on its way to Durango and so was Alfred Donner. Whoever was dead in the freight station, it wasn't Donner.

"You bastard," Johnson said. "I'm coming after you."

Darkness came early in the narrow canyon, but Blake Corley pushed ahead, slowly, cautiously. Several times the hubs of the wagon wheels scraped against the canyon wall as he tried to keep the wagon as far as possible from the precipice that fell away into the Animas River. Only at intervals where the road had been widened to allow converging wagons to pass was it roomy enough that Blake didn't worry about a wheel slipping over the edge. Alfred Donner had been right. This was not like driving a wagon in Kansas.

Blake had ridden the brake lever enough that he could actually smell the burning of the wooden brake shoe against the metal rim. He worried that the brakes might give way and the wagon might overtake the mules, then careen over the cliff.

The mules seemed sluggish and before dark Blake had noticed occasional splotches of blood on the trail. The mules' legs had to be cut and battered from slipping on the trail or stepping through clumps of ice. Blake didn't know what to do. If they stopped, the riders would catch up with them. If they kept going, they could ride over the edge in the darkness. Even if they kept going, the riders would certainly overtake them. When the riders did catch up, Blake knew it would be best to have the wagon secured where they could make a stand rather than get in a running fight where only Moses could return fire. Also, if they stopped Penny could find cover during any shooting.

Finally, Blake drew back on the reins. "It's time we stopped."

Moses cut loose a heavy sigh. "I've been holding my breath for the last half hour, figuring I was going swimming any moment. Blake, you're either a braver or dumber man than I had you figured for."

"I got us this far."

"Only problem is, it ain't far enough. Ain't that right, Missy?"

Penny Heath didn't answer.

"You okay, Missy?"

"Tired and hungry. My stomach's been bothering me."

"Why didn't you say so, Penny? I'd have stopped sooner."

She leaned against Blake's shoulder. "You've got enough to worry about."

Moses stepped out of the wagon on the canyon side of the road. "Blake, I've got about three feet clearance over here. I wouldn't jump down too quickly on your side unless I was sure there was some road beneath me."

"Whatever you say, Mose. Just help Penny down on your side." Blake patted Penny's hand. "You'd better sleep on the road tonight. The mules might spook, if the riders attacked during the night. Mose, why don't you cook us up another can of your frozen peaches."

Penny stood up and edged to Moses. He raised his strong arms to help her over the side.

"Damn poor place to stop the night, Blake, but these steep canyon walls'll keep them from going around us and setting up an ambush down the trail."

Blake locked the brake lever, then twisted the reins around it. He stepped easily over the edge of the wagon, standing on a wheel spoke with one leg and testing the road with the other. He stamped once, then a second time a little father from the wagon. Everything was solid. The third time he tapped at the road, his boot slipped over the edge. "We've got two feet on this side. No more." He stepped off the wheel, then made his way to the back of the wagon, holding onto the sideboard as he went.

He made it around to the wagon tailgate and untied the canvas flap, extracting a blanket and a buffalo robe for Penny. Moses came back to join him.

"Blake," he whispered. "I don't think Missy's well. She seems fevered and weak."

"Damn. We got enough problems without that. How we gonna stand guard and keep an eye on her?"

"I've got my rifle, a pistol, and a box of cartridges. I figure to move back down the road, find me a place to hold them off. You grab the gun belt in my supply sack. That'll give you two guns."

Blake nodded. "If they come, shoot for their mounts. See if we can leave them stranded." Blake grabbed Baldwin's shoulder. "Good luck."

Moses laughed. "Stay away from the edge, will you? I don't think I can drive the wagon if you fell off."

"Hell, Mose, the way you been complaining about my driving, I figured you'd want to handle the team tomorrow."

"I'm scared of heights, Blake." Moses retreated down the road. "When I come in, I'll whistle three times so you don't shoot me."

"That'll be our signal."

Blake watched Moses disappear down the road. Taking the blanket and buffalo robe, he moved to the canyon side of the wagon and found Penny slumped against the granite wall.

"Are you okay? You sure you're just hungry?"

Her only answer was a sob.

He draped the blanket over her shoulders, then patted her on the arm with his gloveless right hand. He fought the urge to kiss her and comfort her, but brushed her cheek instead, feeling her burning flesh.

"You're fevering, aren't you?"

She leaned her head against his chest. The nod of her cheek against his coat was the only answer.

"What is it, Penny?"

She sobbed. "I think I'm losing the baby."

Blake's shoulders sagged and his head dropped against the shawl covering her head. He had never felt more helpless.

"What can I do, Penny? Anything?"

"I don't know," she cried. "Just make me a place to lie down."

Blake kissed the shawl, then squeezed past her, feeling his way along the cliff, trying to find a wide enough spot where she could lie without danger of the wagon running over her should the mules spook. There was none. He hesitated to make a bed behind the wagon for fear she might get hit by gunfire.

He returned to her. "There's no place up ahead for you."

"Anywhere," she pleaded. "Just help me. I feel faint."

"The wagon, then," he said. "It'll be out of the snow."

"Just hurry."

Blake slipped past her, moving to the tailgate and unfastening the canvas, then opening the tailgate. He threw the buffalo robe on the wagon bed and a blanket atop it. He scurried back to Penny and found her slumped on the ground. He picked her up and carried her to the wagon, placing her gently on the buffalo robe and blanket, then pulling them over her.

She moaned.

"Listen, Penny, if the wagon starts moving, or shooting starts, get out, no matter how painful, do you hear me?"

"Yes," she whispered, then moaned again. "My stomach, it hurts so bad." She started crying.

"Penny, I've got to leave for a minute to find Mose. Then I'll be back. I won't leave you for long."

She reached out for him, grabbing his hand and pulling it to her lips. She kissed his hand, then held it to her cheek. "Oh, oh," she cried out, squeezing his hand with surprising strength.

When her grip relaxed, he pulled his hand from hers, then scurried around to the front of the wagon, retrieving Baldwin's supply sack. He shoved his hand inside and felt around, touching a couple cans and what felt like a pair of gloves as well as the gun belt. He pulled out the gun belt and shoved it under his arm, then took the gloves. He removed the glove from his left hand and dropped it in the sack. Quickly, he pulled on the new gloves, then lifted his coat and strapped the gun belt over his own, adjusting it so the extra gun rode in front of his thigh.

He returned to the back of the wagon, patting Penny a final time, then started on the road toward Moses. He walked a ways, then whistled three times.

Moses answered with three short whistles.

Blake moved on, periodically whistling and then narrowing in on the sound of Baldwin's replies.

"Over here," Moses whispered.

Blake found him lying down atop a buffalo robe at the base of the rock wall.

"I thought I heard something down the road," Moses whispered, "until you whistled."

Squatting beside Moses, Blake whispered, "Sorry, Mose, but Penny's in a bad way. She thinks she's losing the baby."

"Lord have mercy."

"I don't know what to do, Mose."

"Wished I could help you, Blake, but that's something I don't know nothing about. Just get back and do what you can to takes care of her. I'll see you aren't bothered none for as long as it takes."

Behind him Blake heard Penny cry out, then scream. A muffled echo repeated the scream down the canyon. Then another voice called out, a voice Blake recognized as Alfred Donner's.

"Blake, Blake Corley," yelled Donner. "What are you doing to that whore?"

Blake patted Moses on the shoulder. "I'll slip back toward

the wagon before I answer so they won't hit you if they shoot at my voice."

"Good luck," Moses answered.

Blake withdrew about twenty yards, clinging to the rock wall.

"Blake Corley, we know you're up ahead," Donner yelled.

"What do you want?" Blake called, expecting a gunshot.

Donner answered, "Just the wagon and team."

"If you wanted it so bad, why didn't you take it to begin with?"

"It don't matter now. Just turn over the wagon and we'll leave you be. If you don't, we'll kill you."

Penny screamed again, her cry piercing the air.

"Damn, Corley, you boys ought to be easier on the whore. Is Black Baldy poking her?"

Blake didn't answer.

"Corley, listen to me, if you want to live. Walk away from the wagon and leave it. We're coming for it at dawn. If you're still around, we'll kill you all."

"If we abandon the wagon, Donner, we have to walk all the way to Durango. You know we can't survive."

Donner laughed. "Only a fool would've tried to get a wagon to Durango in this weather to begin with. Cut a couple of the mules loose and ride them, if you like, just leave the damn wagon."

"Penny can't ride and she can't walk. We'll be here come morning."

"Enjoy it, Blake, it'll be the last morning you ever see."

17

At the sound of Penny's moans, Blake Corley made his way to
the wagon, crouching low beside the rock wall.

"Blake?" Penny cried. "The pain comes in waves. I'm thirsty."

Blake knew they had no water and even if they did, it
would be frozen. "Snow's the best I can do, Penny."

She gasped at a spasm of pain, then breathed furiously as
her body writhed on the buffalo robe.

Squatting beside her, Blake cupped a handful of snow in
his hands and placed it at her lips.

She shoved his hands away, cried out in pain, then fell limp.

"Now," she whimpered.

Blake touched the snow to her lips and she took it in her
mouth.

She sighed, then contorted as another wave of pain shot
through her stomach. "It hurts so."

Blake stroked her hair.

"I ran away so they wouldn't kill the baby and now I've
killed it." She sobbed.

Patting her hand, Blake bent over and kissed her on the
cheek. "It'll be okay." He hoped he was right.

"I killed the baby," she kept repeating between moans of agony.

"Penny, don't blame yourself, please. There's nothing you could've done." He stroked her cheek and could feel the warm tears streaming down her skin. He had never felt more helpless.

He stayed at her side for more than an hour, calming her, allowing her to squeeze his hand at each shudder of pain. Then she quit sobbing and moaning as the pain subsided. She lay quiet and still, her breath the only sound. When she spoke, she seemed embarrassed. "I've bled a lot. It must be cleaned."

Blake nodded. "I'll get you something to clean with."

"No, Blake, I'm too weak."

Blake grimaced. "Let me see if I can find something."

"Please."

He shoved his hand in his coat pocket for a neckerchief or anything that might work, then moved around to the front of the wagon and grabbed Baldwin's flour sack. He shoved his hand inside, not expecting to find anything of help, but he felt a couple lengths of woolen cloth among the frozen cans. As he pulled out the cloth, he realized he had found Baldwin's spare socks.

He returned to Penny's side. "I found some socks." He held them to his nose. "They smell new. It's just that I don't know if I can do this."

She reached out and grabbed his hand. "Other men have seen me."

"But they didn't care for you in the same way I do."

"You didn't want to bring me to begin with."

"Because I didn't want to see you hurt or worse."

"Come to me," she said.

Blake bent over her cheek.

She lifted her head and kissed him for a moment. "No man ever treated me so well." She struggled to pull back the robe and the blanket. Then she reached for her skirt and pulled it up.

Blake was glad it was so dark that he could not see. She lifted her hips momentarily so he could remove her undergarment.

Her drawers were blood-soaked. He threw the undergarment aside, then took the socks and began to clean her as best he could, wiping between her legs and then down her thighs. He could tell she had lost considerable blood and knew she would be weak for a few days. Why couldn't this have happened later? Why now when Alf Donner and his men were within range?

"That's the best I can do," he said.

"That's fine. I've a few undergarments in my valise."

Blake eased to the wagon, untied the tarp, and groped for her valise. It wasn't within reach. Still embarrassed by having to clean Penny, he marched back around the back of the wagon, swinging wide of the rear wheel.

Then he remembered. The narrow ledge!

His left boot slipped over the precipice.

He gasped.

"Blake," cried Penny, suddenly alarmed.

His right foot caught on a stone, then slid toward the edge.

Blake fell backwards, his feet slipping out from under him and over the cliff. He fell hard, but the snow softened his landing. His arms flailed wildly.

"Blake!" screamed Penny.

His hand hit the tailgate, brushed against the rear wagon wheel. He was sliding over the edge.

His fingers caught the wheel rim, breaking his slide for a moment.

Blake tried to roll over and thrust his right hand toward the wheel.

His waist slipped over the edge.

He caught his breath as the fingers of his right hand wrapped firmly around a wheel spoke.

"Blake, Blake, what happened? Answer me. Please, God, don't let him fall."

The mules stamped nervously and Blake felt the wheel turn a fraction as they pulled against the brake and the wheel wedges he had set.

His hands stopped the fall, though his legs dangled over the cliff.

Taking a deep breath, Blake tightened his hold on the spoke, then began to pull himself back atop the ledge. He managed to get his legs, then his feet firmly on the road, then knelt on his knees, clinging to the wheel and shaking like a leaf in a breeze.

"Blake, Blake."

"I slipped."

"I know. I don't know what I would've done had you fallen."

Blake stayed where he was until he quit shaking, then he managed to get to his feet and walk on wobbly knees to the front of the wagon. He untied the tarp and quickly found her valise. He held it in one hand and grasped the wagon side-board as he returned to Penny.

"Maybe you should get what you need." He handed her the bag.

She opened it and dug for a pair of drawers. Once again, she asked for his help to get them on. He assisted, then straightened her dress. He covered her with the blanket and buffalo robe.

"You need to get your rest."

"And you yours," she replied.

Blake took the extra blanket from the back and wrapped it around his shoulders, then marched to the rock wall. He leaned against it, then slipped down until he sat on the packed snow. He needed rest, but he also knew he must sleep lightly if he did sleep at all.

The longer he tried to get a little shut-eye, the harder it seemed in coming. While he had been scared for Penny, he had not noticed the cold, nor the stiff breeze blowing through the canyon. Now the world never seemed colder. When he finally found rest, he could not be certain whether he had fallen asleep or had frozen to death.

His sleep was shattered at dawn by a gunshot.

18

The clouds were thick and the early morning light was dim as Blake Corley jumped to his feet, slapping at his thigh for one of the pistols he wore. He tossed his blanket in the back of the wagon. Down the road, another shot cut through the air then pinged off the granite rock.

"They're coming," yelled Moses Baldwin.

Blake ran to Penny Heath, hurriedly patting her on the shoulder. She was slow to answer and sluggish when she did. Blake pulled back the buffalo robe and blanket covering her face. She was pale. He lifted her arm and it fell weakly to her side. Her eyes fluttering for a moment, she seemed to wake up and smile, then her eyelids closed.

Blake glanced back over his shoulder at the sound of another gunshot. "Stay down," he said, then headed toward the gunfire. The snow crunched beneath his feet as he moved in a crouch, gun in hand, clinging to the sheer wall. In front of him, he finally saw Baldwin stretched out on a buffalo robe, his Winchester pointing toward Silverton.

Blake whistled three times and Moses lifted his head

enough to look over his shoulder. He waved his arm for Blake to approach.

Blake scurried to Baldwin, throwing himself on the robe and pointing his gun at the danger.

"There's three of them," Moses announced. "Two of them I saw hiding the bodies. The third, I don't know."

"That's Alfred Donner, the freight agent. He was the one tormenting us last night."

"They started down the road this morning on foot. I drove them back with a couple shots. How's Missy."

"I'm worried about her. She's pale and feeble. Lost a lot of blood during the night."

"Think she could ride one of the mules?"

Blake shook his head. "She's too tired."

"Watch it," Moses shouted, then squeezed off a shot.

Blake saw a head duck back behind a rock.

"That was the one-eyed fellow. I've been aiming to put out his other eye."

"How many times you shot, Mose?"

"Five or six, I reckon."

"We don't have ammunition to last very long at this rate."

"Any better ideas, Blake?"

"If we stay, we run out of ammunition. We might just as well get in the wagon and ride. You cover our backside and I'll drive." Blake glanced up at the clouds. "Looks like we could get more snow."

"I ain't got a better idea, Blake. Go get the wagon ready and I'll come running when you holler."

Blake holstered his pistol, then scrambled toward the wagon. He scooped Penny from the ground quickly as he carried her to the wagon box, lowering her down on the floor. Then he kicked the rock wedges from beneath the wheels and climbed into the seat, careful not to step on Penny lying beneath him on the floorboard. He untied the reins, then wrapped them tightly around his wrists. He released the brake lever until he felt the wagon start to inch forward. "Come on, Mose," he yelled.

Blake heard a gunshot, then silence before the sound of feet running through the glazed snow. He glanced over his shoulder and saw Baldwin charging hard for the wagon, carrying the rifle in one hand and the buffalo robe in the other. Blake released the brake lever fully and shook the reins, the mules began to pull the wagon.

The footfalls grew louder, then Blake heard a clatter as Moses tossed his rifle in the back. He felt the wagon lurch as Moses grabbed hold of the tailgate and jerked himself aboard.

"You okay?" Blake yelled.

"Damn right. Where's Missy?"

There was as much concern in Baldwin's voice for Penny as there was worry about himself, Blake thought. "She's up here on the floorboard."

"You protect her, now." Baldwin grabbed his rifle and twisted around in the wagon, aiming the weapon at their attackers. "There they come," he shouted.

Blake glanced back over his shoulder, then jerked the team hard to his right when he got too close to the ledge.

"You watch the driving and I'll watch our friends. They're following nice and easy. If they gain on us, I'll try to pick one off or knock a mule out from under them."

"We'll be okay, Mose, until we get out of this canyon. Then they can circle around us and ambush us along the route."

The clouds began to drop intermittent flakes of snow.

"Don't let it snow too much," Moses said, "or they'll move in closer. Hey, they stopped. Maybe they're giving up."

Before Blake could express his doubts, he heard Alfred Donner calling.

"Corley, your only chance is to give up the wagon."

"Thought this morning was our last chance to surrender and live. We didn't surrender and we're still alive."

"Give up the wagon, Blake."

"Can't do it, Donner. Got to carry the girl to Durango."

Donner didn't answer for a minute. "Leave the coffins and then take her to Durango."

"Thought you wanted the coffins to get to their next of kin."

Donner's shrill laugh echoed through the canyon. "They don't have any kin."

Blake couldn't make sense of it. "You can have them all when we reach Durango, Donner, not before."

"Here they come again," Moses whispered. "Slow down a bit and let them gain on me. Maybe they'll get close enough so I can wing one of them."

Blake touched the brake lever.

Moses said, "Try this, you loud-mouth dog."

Blake flinched at the explosion of Moses's rifle, then grinned. By the thud of the bullet, Blake knew the lead had struck flesh. "Good shot, Mose."

"I was aiming for the talker, but got his mule. That'll keep them a ways back."

Blake glanced over his shoulder and saw a mule down and kicking. He saw Donner scrambling to his feet and shaking his fist.

"You'll die for that," Donner yelled.

"Pick up the pace," Moses said. "Maybe we can distance ourselves from them."

Blake eased off on the brake and the wagon leaned into the mules, causing one to stumble before catching its feet. The animals began to pull into the harnesses and give the wagon some speed. The wagon bounced over a rock hidden beneath the snow. The wagon seemed to be gaining too much speed and Blake pushed the brake lever, the wooden shoe screeched against the metal wheel rim and began to smoke. The wagon slowed, then lurched ahead, a wheel mule stumbled and the wagon shuddered, but the harness kept him from falling. The mules were terrified as the wagon gained momentum.

"Whoa, whoa," Blake screamed, shoving his boot against the floorboard to maintain his own balance.

Penny cried out.

Blake realized he had stepped on Penny's leg. He lifted his boot, then slammed it against the wooden footrest. "Whoa, whoa."

The wagon slowed. Blake fought the reins, finally bringing the wagon to a stop, near the edge of the road. Blake looked down at the Animas River fifty feet below, the water rushing by.

"Don't look down on my side of the wagon," Blake said to Moses.

"It don't matter, I got my eyes closed and I've been flapping my arms to see if I could fly."

Blake twisted around on the seat and glanced behind him. Donner and his two men had stopped to watch. Donner was mounted again, apparently saddling the pack mule to replace his downed mount.

"How's Missy?" Moses asked. "I heard her scream."

"I stepped on her foot," Blake admitted.

"Wish you'd stepped on the brake."

Blake let loose a deep breath and realized he was trembling, but he could no longer tell if it was from the close call or the cold. He stared down the canyon, then cursed at what he saw. They were emerging from the canyon. The road made a wide curve against the canyon wall, then fell down a sharp incline until it was almost at the level of the river itself. They were doubly cursed. The brakes might not hold and they would careen into the wall or over the edge into the river. Even if they made it safely to the water's edge, the road followed the wide tree-lined skirt of another, gentler mountain. Once the wagon descended down the road and emerged from the canyon, Donner and his two men could follow, then circle ahead of the wagon for an ambush anywhere along the way to Durango.

Moses stood up and looked over Blake's shoulder at the road ahead. "What do you think, Blake?"

Shaking his head, Blake replied, "You better start flapping your arms again, Mose."

"Can I close my eyes?"

"If you can fly, you can."

Moses shrugged. "A man's got to die sometime. At least I won't die a slave."

"The cliff road's been our ally until now, Mose. Once we reach the river our only protection will be our ammunition."

"And, we're running out of it, Blake."

"Take your seat, Mose, we're heading through."

Baldwin sat back down, holding his rifle tight in one fist and the sideboard with the other.

Blake rattled the reins, then released the brake slowly, allowing the mules to pull into the harness before the wagon began to gather momentum. Blake gritted his teeth. The mules started at a walk, then moved into a trot as they hit the incline. Faster and faster the mules began to run, the wagon chasing them down the road. Blake tugged on the reins, then slammed his foot against the brake.

The lever went limp.

Blake tugged back on the reins, but it had no effect on the mules.

The wagon was out of control.

19

"The sons of bitches," cried Luther Perry, lifting his rifle to shoot at the wagon.

Alfred Donner grabbed the rifle barrel and shoved it away. "Don't fire until I tell you to. You understand, Luther?"

Luther grumbled. "Why not? I'm cold and ready to end this."

"You want to be rich or not, Luther?"

Perry nodded.

Donner pointed to the wagon. "That damn Kansas flatlander is having a hard enough time getting that freight wagon down the road. If you shot him or your gunfire spooked the mules, the wagon'd go over the edge and that would be the end of our fortune."

Perry scratched his head and lifted his rifle, cradling the barrel in the crook of his arm. "If we don't get them, they'll be all the way to Durango and we'll still be as broke as now."

Donner spat in the snow. "Luther, you ain't got the sense God gave a rock. At the bottom of the incline, the road levels out by the river and the terrain'll be easier driving for a while and more opportunity for us to circle them."

"I say we get them now."

Donner shrugged. "Either do what I say or head back to Silverton. Don't you still want to get that black son of a bitch who killed Bibb?"

"Damn right."

Donner turned to Dick Pincham. "You ain't saying much."

"I don't have much to say."

"Once they reach the river," Donner said, "we'll circle into the trees and get ahead of them, find a place where we can ambush them."

Pincham laughed. "You ain't too anxious to get within rifle range of that wagon again, are you? If he'd been a better shot he'd killed you instead of your mule. Had that happened, Luther and I'd get a bigger share of the loot, now wouldn't we?"

Donner's eyes narrowed and his gaze fixed on Pincham. "What are you getting at?"

"Just making an observation."

"Sounded more like a threat to me."

Pincham raised his nose, sniffing the air, and stared arrogantly at Donner. "How'd you say Bibb Clack died?"

"The damned darkie got him."

Pincham grinned. "Bibb walked all the way to the freight station after he was shot? Went to you instead of a doctor? Got all the way into town without anybody seeing him wounded and needing help."

"What are you getting at, Dick?"

"Yeah," said Perry, echoing Donner.

Pincham's face widened into a cynical smile. "Just what a strong, brave man our friend Bibb Clack was."

Perry nodded. "That's right."

Donner spat in the snow again. He knew Pincham was playing games with him, knew that Pincham had his doubts and, most of all, knew he would have to kill Pincham after they got the money and before they reached Durango.

Pincham pointed down the trail. "Our fortune has started to move again."

"We've got time to catch up with them."

"Not if the snow gets so bad we can't see."

Donner spat again. "You keep forgetting who's in charge here, Dick."

Pincham cocked his head and stared hard at Donner. "And, I keep remembering whose stupid idea it was to try and slip the money out of Silverton this way."

Donner pointed his finger at Pincham. "It wouldn't have been a problem if you and Perry hadn't been spotted burying Barney and Pug."

"Once we get the money, Alf, I'm through taking orders from you. I'm taking my share and getting as far away from you as I can and spend my money when and where I want."

"Yeah," said Perry.

"Until then," Donner nodded, "you just remember who's in charge of things." He nudged his mule forward. Donner considered throwing his gun on Pincham and killing him, but decided against it until they had the money in hand. Pincham seemed to understand Bibb Clack's true fate. That made him a dangerous man. Perry wasn't as shrewd as Pincham, so he wasn't as dangerous. But Perry was too dumb a man to deserve a share of the money. Donner figured he would have to kill them both before they reached Durango.

Donner watched the freight wagon as it began to inch down the cliff road. The snow had picked up and the wagon was partially obscured through the white veil. He clinched his jaw, hoping Blake Corley had what it took to get the wagon down the cliff road where the canyon narrows broadened into a wide mountain slope. Donner glanced over his shoulder at his motionless confederates. He motioned for them to start down the road.

Pincham grinned. "Go ahead, Alf. We'll be right behind you."

Donner nodded to Perry. "Why don't you lead us for awhile, Luther?"

Perry shook his head vigorously. "I don't want him shooting my mule out from under me."

"What about you taking the lead, Dick?"

Pincham grinned. "I don't want you riding at my back, Alf."

Donner drew his coat sleeve across his lips, then looked toward the wagon. It seemed to be gathering too much speed. "Dammit," he cried. "If Corley can't slow her down, it'll run off the cliff and we'll still be poor men."

"Poor men, thanks to your damn fool idea," Pincham answered with disgust.

20

Blake Corley kicked at the brake lever.

It was useless.

He tugged on the reins, but the mules could not stop on the steep grade. Their hooves slashed at the snow, kicking up bits of ice that pelted Blake's face.

"Hold on," Blake screamed as he saw a curve in the road rushing toward him.

Almost instantly, the wagon hit the bend. Corley jerked the reins hard to the right, then slowly to the left as he tried to steer the wagon around the curve.

The hub of the rear wheel brushed against the side wall, jolting the wagon.

The wagon careened toward the ledge.

With all his strength, Blake jerked the reins hard to the right again, but the mules answered the wagon's building momentum more than his steering.

The wagon hit a rock in the road and bounced up, then landed with a jarring impact that broke the line securing one of the coffins. The coffin slid to the front of the wagon bed.

"Do something," yelled Moses.

The wagon edged back toward the canyon wall, the rear hub hitting the wall and jarring the wagon.

Blake tugged on the reins again, then threw them aside. They were useless. If he didn't act fast, the wagon would go over the ledge or throw them all into the rock wall.

Blake stood up.

Penny screamed.

Blake leaped from the wagon box toward the mule in front of him. Blake hit hard against the animal's back, then clawed at the harness for a hold. As his fingers slipped around the leather, he tried to grab the halter and stop this animal as if that might have some effect on the other five charging mules.

Nothing worked, the wagon kept barreling ahead, threatening to overtake the mules and run them under.

In desperation, Blake swatted at his hip, jerking his coat up and slapping at a pistol in one of the holsters around his waist.

Behind him he heard the shouts of both Moses and Penny.

He jerked the pistol free, then pointed at the head of the lunging mule to his right. He cocked the hammer, then aimed for a spot right beneath the mule's ear.

Blake gritted his teeth, then squeezed the trigger.

The mule collapsed to the ground, the harness dragging the carcass for a minute, then snapping.

The front wheel ran over the carcass, jarring the wagon and jerking the other mules hard in their harnesses. Blake was thrown forward, landing hard against the mule's neck, losing his pistol and bruising his left shoulder while somehow managing to hold his grip on the harness.

The wagon braked, but its momentum swung the left rear wheel over the edge of the cliff. The second coffin snapped free and flew against the tailgate. Moses lost his grip on the sideboard and was thrown against the coffin, the extra weight on that side of the wagon bed tipped that corner of the wagon toward the canyon. The rear axle snapped when it crashed down on the granite ledge.

Moses lost his grip on his rifle and felt it slide toward his feet. He grabbed for it, then felt the wagon teeter toward the canyon below. He threw his head back against the wagon bed, lowered his chin against his chest and looked between his boots which rested upon the tailgate. Through the cracks in the wood, he could see the rushing waters of the Animas River far below.

Very carefully, he slid his hand along the plank floor and wrapped his fingers around the barrel of the rifle. With his every move, the wagon seemed to slip toward the canyon.

"Blake," he called softly, "my eyes are open and I've got a problem."

"I stopped the damn thing," Blake answered, twisting about to look at the wagon. He gasped at what he saw.

The rear corner of the wagon dangled over the cliff. The wagon seemed precariously balanced.

Blake heard Penny moan, then he grimaced when he saw her head slowly rise from the driver's box. The whole wagon seemed to quiver.

"Don't move, Penny."

She seemed confused. She looked at Blake, then at the wagon. Her eyes widened with fear.

"We've got a problem," Blake said.

"Damn right we do," answered Moses. "I can't fly."

Blake worked his hand from beneath the harness and slid off his mule, stepping over the contorted neck of the mule he had shot.

"What happened?" Penny asked, unable to disguise the fear in her voice.

Blake eased to the end of the wagon, glancing warily up the grade at the three Donner men who seemed torn between charging the wagon or holding back for fear it might fall over the edge. Blake didn't understand. This was the perfect opportunity for them to attack, yet they held back.

"Don't unlatch the tailgate," Moses called softly.

Confident that Donner wouldn't try anything for a moment,

Blake glanced into the back of the wagon and saw one coffin and Baldwin wedged against the dangling corner. The other coffin, as best Blake could see under the canvas tarp, was caught between the head of the first and the back of the driver's box.

Blake slipped to the rear of the wagon, grabbed the sideboard and tried to pull the wagon away from the edge, but the wagon weighed too much. "Listen to me, Mose. Try to move toward me. I'll hold the wheel and steady it."

Moses sighed, then edged toward Blake.

The wagon quivered.

"Ohhhh," Moses said softly.

"Just take it easy, Mose," Blake said, then turned to the front of the wagon. "Penny, slide to the canyon side of the box. Maybe that will help out." Blake gripped the wagon as firmly as he could. "Now Mose."

Moses inched across the wagon bed, dragging his rifle. Blake felt the wagon quiver as Baldwin slid toward him.

"I may not need to fly after all," Moses said as he lifted his rifle for Blake.

Blake eased his grip on the wagon. It seemed stable so he grabbed the rifle and glanced down toward Donner and his men watching through the snow.

Moses started to climb over the sideboard, but Blake shook his head. "Pull the coffins to this side and put more weight on firm ground."

"Lord have mercy, I think you do want to see me fly." Cautiously, Moses reached and grabbed a handle on the nearest coffin. He started to drag it across the wagon bed. "Something funny about this coffin." He worked it to the near sideboard then reached for the second. "This one, too." He pulled it across the wagon, let loose a sigh of relief, then crawled over the side. "I never was so glad to have my feet on firm ground." He looked at the dead mule, bent down, and inspected the axle, then shook his head. "We've got more problems than a sinner at prayer meeting."

"We've still got five mules," Blake replied.

"Missy can't ride and the wagon won't go."

"I'm not planning on staying the winter." Blake glanced back down the road and thought Donner's men were advancing. He lifted his rifle and the three stopped cold, then backed their mules up.

"We've got to repair the wagon then."

"No way to do it."

Moses scoffed. "I lived in Alabama during the war. You learned to make do. What tools we got?"

Blake pointed to the opposite side of the wagon. "The toolbox is over there. Better start flapping your arms."

Baldwin gulped. "You wouldn't make me do that, now would you?"

"I guess not. As much as you weigh, you might tip the wagon over." Blake handed Moses the rifle. "Keep this handy, but hold on to the wagon while I fetch our tools." Blake eased into the wagon, stepping on the nearest coffin, then sliding onto the wagon bed. He moved cautiously to the other side, then bent over the edge to open the toolbox. He could see the Animas River below as he lifted the latch and lid, then pulled out a hammer, a shovel, a four-foot crosscut saw, an ax, a mallet, a wagon jack, a wrench, a twelve-foot length of chain, and a can of nails, nuts, and bolts. He made two trips across the wagon bed, tossing the tools onto the road. Then he fetched the supply sacks and Penny's valise, carrying them with him as he climbed down from the wagon.

Dropping the sacks, he picked up the jack and wrench, that doubled as a jack handle, then moved to the back of the wagon. He slipped the jack beneath the wagon bed as close as possible to the ledge then used the wrench to jack up the rear wheel. "It's steady now."

"The mules are fidgeting," Moses said. "We need to check them."

"Let's unload the coffins. Set them up in the road for

cover and one of us can stand watch." Blake unhooked the tail-gate and grabbed a handle on the rear coffin. He dragged it halfway out, then motioned for Moses to assist.

As they removed it, the coffin sagged in their hands, its weight oddly distributed. "I see what you mean, Mose."

From down the road, Blake heard Donner call. "What are you doing?"

Blake looked to Mose and shook his head. "What the hell difference does it make?"

"Corley," Donner yelled. "What are you planning to do with the coffin?"

"Gonna throw it over the edge," Blake shouted.

"No, no," Donner screamed. "We'll stay back."

Moses shrugged. "Hell, these fellows is already dead."

Blake guided the coffin to the middle of the road and sat it down in the snow. He looked over his shoulder and the three men were retreating. It didn't make sense. He moved back to the wagon and climbed inside to slide out the next coffin. This coffin too seemed oddly loaded. Moses helped him carry it to the middle of the road and place it atop the first one. Blake assigned Moses to stand watch with the rifle, then went to check on Penny and the mules.

As he neared the driver's box, it struck him. He turned about and ran back to Moses, grabbing him by the shoulder.

"What's gotten into you, Blake?"

"Tell me, Mose, why these men started after you?"

"I told you, I saw them hiding a couple bodies."

"I knew it and I know what's in these coffins."

"The men killed in the robbery?"

"No, sir, the stolen money. Donner and his men were behind it. There may be a hundred thousand dollars in those coffins."

Moses shrugged. "Even if you're right, all the money in the world's not gonna get us off this mountain."

21

Moses Baldwin was right, Blake Corley agreed. With Penny still down, they didn't have many options and money wouldn't help with anything, unless they could burn it for heat. Blake glanced back up the road. Donner and his men had disappeared, but Blake could not be certain if it was because they had retreated or the snowfall had increased.

"See any sign of them, Mose?"

"Not a bit."

Blake plucked the tools from the snow and carried them to the coffins where he propped the ax, shovel, and saw, then deposited the hammer, chain, and can of nails on top. Blake retreated to check on Penny. He found her hunkered down on the floorboard, covered with the buffalo robe.

He stroked her cheek with his fingers. She stirred.

"How are you feeling?"

"Tired," she said. "Maybe I've bled a little more, but I think its all stopped. We're not gonna make it, are we?"

"We'll do fine, somehow."

"I'm holding you back, aren't I?"

Blake shrugged.

"You and Mose could just ride away if it weren't for me. I should've never left. I lost the baby because of it. Will kill the two of you as a result and then I'll freeze to death myself before it's all over."

"How's Missy doing?" Moses called. "Tell her she wasn't sleeping with no dead men after all."

Penny shook her head. "What's he talking about?"

"We think the coffins hold the money from the robbery the other day. Donner backed off when we bluffed about throwing them over the cliff. He wouldn't care about the bodies, just money."

"If we left the money, would they leave us along?" she asked, a hopeful lilt in her hoarse voice.

Blake shook his head. "Now they need to kill us even more, so we can't tell anyone."

"Won't our luck ever change?"

Blake ran his fingers through her hair. "My luck changed when I met you."

"Must have turned for the bad."

"No, for the better, even with all of this. You stay warm while I check on the mules, then we'll figure out some grub for you to eat, see if you can't get back some strength in case you need to ride."

She groaned. "I can't ride."

"Then you won't, even if I have to carry you all the way to Durango."

Blake left her to inspect the mules. They stamped and fidgeted as much from the dead mule as from the weather or the proximity to the ledge. The mules seemed as fine as could be expected in the frigid weather. He hoped the harness had not snapped when he shot the mule, though he wouldn't know for sure until he unbuckled it from the carcass wedged beneath the front wheel.

He marched to Moses, who stood with his rifle pointed back up the grade. "Haven't seen a sign of them."

"If we don't keep moving, we're dead, Mose."

Moses tapped the saw and ax. "Least we won't freeze."

Blake cocked his head and stared askance at Baldwin. "There's a stone wall on one side of us, a cliff on the other, three men that want to kill us on our tail and not a tree within reach."

"Wagon's worthless, Blake, so we might just as well use it for firewood." Then Moses laughed. "By damn, I've figured how to get us down from here. Missy, too."

"Huh?"

Baldwin shoved the rifle in Blake's hands. "You stay here and watch for Donner." He grabbed the saw and marched to the wagon, then crawled in the back.

Blake's gaze bounced back and forth between Moses and the road. To Blake's surprise, Baldwin eased toward the far side of the wagon. He untied the front half of the tarp and jerked it free of the sideboards, then moved back from the ledge side, stopping an arm's length away. He raised the saw and dropped it on the sideboard, then began to push and pull the tool, its teeth biting into the wood.

"I'll be damned," Blake said. "I thought you were afraid of heights, Mose."

"I got my eyes closed."

"But, Mose, what the hell are you doing?"

"Gonna turn this wagon into a cart."

"Well, I'll be double damned."

"Way, I figure it, Blake, I'll saw this damned thing in half and we can make it down the road and find us a better place to fort up."

"You're pretty good with a saw."

"Beats an ax, Blake. I never manned a saw I didn't like."

Baldwin's powerful arm moved back and forth, rhythmically, steadily, the noise becoming a constant rasp. At the sudden stop of the noise, Blake turned around to see Moses shucking his coat, then attacking the wagon again.

Blake watched the road for signs of Donner until his eyeballs were sore. Then he picked up the hammer atop the coffin and removed the ax, chain, and can of nails and bolts. Propping the rifle against the stacked coffins, he used the claw end of the hammer to work open the nailed lid of the cheap wooden box. He knew he'd feel foolish if he found a body inside, but he had to satisfy his curiosity. It would explain a lot of things. Gradually, he worked the lid up careful not to damage it. He saw what he suspected. Two strongboxes had been strapped inside. "We were right, Mose. It is the money."

Blake used the hammer to jerk the leather straps from the screws that were holding the strongboxes, then lifted both out and carried them to the wagon. Going back to the coffins, he pushed the empty one aside and pried open the lid of the second. Just as before he found two more strongboxes, though one had slipped its leather straps. He loosened the straps on the other, then carried both strongboxes to the wagon.

Keeping an eye up the road, Blake kicked around in the snow, seeking rocks he could replace inside the coffins. He spent about thirty minutes collecting the rocks then loading them in the coffins. and renailing the lids. He didn't expect the ruse to fool Donner and his two men, but he figured it might buy a little more time, and time was what he needed.

When the rasp of the saw stopped, Blake glanced at Moses who wiped his brow, then picked up his coat and covered his shoulders.

"Need a breather."

Blake walked over to the wagon and inspected Baldwin's work. He was about halfway through the thick planks of the wagon bed.

"Another hour and this'll be done," Moses said, pointing to the strongboxes in the snow. "You're damn smart, Blake Corley."

"Not smart enough to figure we could cut the wagon in half and get down from here."

"I'm doing it for Missy."

"Hell, Mose, you're doing it because you can't fly."

"And you can't drive or we wouldn't be in this fix."

Both men laughed a moment, then Moses picked up the saw and touched the blade. "She's still warm," he said. "Only thing I can't figure out is whether the damn wagon box will slide around the axle and tip over. This wagon has a drop tongue. We've got to figure out a way to steady."

"There's a chain with the tools. I can hook it between the wagon box and the undercarriage. That should keep it from tipping over."

"You're getting smarter all the time, Blake." Moses let the coat drop from his shoulders, then slid the saw back into the floorboard and began to attack the planks again.

Blake checked the road and saw no sign of Donner or his men. He retreated to the coffins, took the chain and a couple nuts and bolts from the tin can and moved to the front of the wagon. He secured the chain to the undercarriage's center brace, then bolted the top of the chain to an eyebolt in the front of the wagon box.

He returned to the coffins, picked up the other tools and laid them in the back of the wagon behind the driver's box. He gathered the supply sacks and dropped them into the wagon on the remaining blankets and buffalo robes.

By his heaving breath, Blake knew Moses was tiring fast so he offered to help, but Moses turned him down.

"I finish what I start. You can remove the tailgate so we can nail it over the new end here."

Blake checked the road. Seeing nothing he moved to the tailgate, unhooked the chains, then slipped the gate from its hinges and carried it toward the front.

Moses jumped out of the wagon bed and began to saw into the remaining sideboard. "There's one plank uncut in the wagon bed," he explained. "Once I get this side done, it won't take but a minute to finish that plank."

"If this works, Mose, you're damn smart yourself."

"If it don't, we're dead."

Moses quickly cut through the thinner sideboard, then attacked the final plank. The wood creaked, then snapped as the saw broke through. The rear of the wagon fell to the ground. The front of the wagon tipped backward but an inch before the chain caught and held it in place.

"You're damn smart, Mose, and we ain't dead yet."

Moses grabbed the tailgate and held it to the back of the wagon, while Blake got the hammer and nails. He quickly nailed it in place.

Blake pointed to the rifle at the coffins. "Stand guard while I re-rig the harness."

Moses grabbed his coat and pulled it on, buttoning it up quickly as he retreated to the coffins to watch the mountain road obscured in the flurry of snow up the canyon.

Blake examined the two lead mules and released one whose legs were badly cut up. The animal trotted on down the mountain road and disappeared in the snowfall. Moving back to the wagon, he removed the lines on the downed mule then unhooked the remaining lead mule and backed him into the place of the dead mule. Smelling blood, the mule kicked the carcass and stamped as Blake hooked him to the wagon.

"I figure you and me ride a mule since we don't have any brakes. You still got your knife?"

Moses grunted.

"Then let me borrow it."

Baldwin carried his knife to Blake.

"I'm cutting the lines on each of the mules to make reins. One of us'll ride the lead pair and the other'll ride the wheelers."

"Give me the leather straps in case we need them later."

Blake went from mule to mule cutting the lines and tying the ends to make a set of reins for each animal. He tossed the severed leathers to Moses who threw them in back of the wagon.

"Load up the strongboxes, Mose. It'd be a damn shame to leave the money for Donner."

After placing the strongboxes in the wagon, Moses surveyed

the area, picking up the hammer and can of nails Blake had left behind the wagon.

Blake returned Moses's knife. "Keep up with this because I've got a hunger for some frozen peaches."

"Is that everything we'll need?"

"Except the coffins."

"I hope we won't need them."

"Then let's see if this contraption will work, Blake."

The two men mounted mules, Moses crawling atop the lead mule on the canyon side and Blake settling on the wheeler on the river side.

"Ready, Mose?"

"Let's go."

"Hi-ya," Blake yelled.

The mules stepped forward, tugging into their harnesses to drag the wheel over the now frozen body of the dead mule. When the cart rolled over the body, it shoved against the team and for an instant Blake thought the animals would stumble out of control. Both he and Moses jerked on the reins and the animals kept their feet.

Slowly, gradually, the cart wound its way down the steep grade. Blake glanced over his shoulder, but saw no sign of Donner.

He heard a stirring behind him in the wagon box, then a gasp.

"Blake, Mose," called Penny's hoarse voice. "The wagon's rolling."

"It's okay, Penny," Blake answered.

She lifted her head and smiled to see Blake.

"I feared it had gotten away from you."

"No, everything is fine. Once the road bottoms out, we'll fix something to eat and ride until dark. We'll find us a place to fort up and then tomorrow maybe we can get to Durango."

"If this snow, lets up," called Moses. "If this snow ever lets up."

22

"We should've attacked them while we were close, Alf." Dick Pincham lifted his eye patch and scratched the pit where his left eye had been.

Alfred Donner pointed at Pincham. "They'd have thrown the coffins over the cliff and this'd all been for nothing. Then where'd we be?"

Pincham grinned. "Just as broke as we are right now, Alf. Only thing worse than being broke would be being broke and dead like Bibb."

"Shut up? We'll get them tomorrow."

"Hell, they'll be gone by then. You've heard the noise up there. I'm not sure what they've been doing, but it's nothing that'll work to our advantage."

"It's a couple hours until dark. Then we can sneak up on them and take our shots, Dick."

"Hell, Alf, the way it's been snowing we could've gotten close enough to shoot them long time ago."

"We'll wait until first dark."

"Dammit, Alf, every decision you've made's been the wrong one. A damn idiot could've made better choices."

Donner squared around to face Pincham. "Maybe we should just settle this right now."

Pincham unbuttoned his coat to uncover his gun.

Luther Perry jumped between the two men. "Hold on. How can you think about fighting as cold as it is? Once we get the money, we're gonna be sitting pretty. Buy anything we want, have women wanting us, you name it. We'll eat something and come tomorrow we'll catch up with them."

"Luther," said Pincham, "you ain't as dumb as Alf's been saying you are."

"What?" Luther spun around to Donner. "What've you been saying?"

"Nothing, Luther, can't you see he's just trying to turn you against me."

Pincham laughed. "Alf's gonna try to pick us off, you and me, Luther, like he killed Bibb."

Perry stared hard at Donner. "Is that so?"

Donner shook his head. Pincham was a shrewd one. The sooner Donner killed him, the better. "Hell, no, Luther. Why'd I kill someone like Bibb?"

"For a bigger share of the loot, Alf. You and I both know that."

"You boys don't forget. If it wasn't for me, neither of you'd have a chance at any of this money. I'm what's given you a chance to have real money in your pocket, more than you'll ever get for day wages."

"We ain't got the money yet, Alf, and there's no argument about that," Pincham said.

"None of us have, Dick, and that includes me. And when we get the money, we best go our own ways right then or we're gonna kill each other."

Perry threw up his hands. "I don't know which of you to believe."

Pincham pointed to Perry's shoulder. "A bit of advice, Luther. From here on in, you better watch your back or Alf's liable to put a couple holes in it. Did you shoot Bibb in the back, Alf?"

"Damn you, Dick," Donner said, spinning about and heading to his hobbled mule. "Eat something for supper, both of you, because as soon as it's dark we'll slip down and ambush them."

"They'll be gone by the time we get there, Alf," Pincham challenged.

"You saw the wagon, broken axle and all. They're not going anywhere."

"Alf, they've got mules, don't you understand. They can up and ride away."

"So what if they do that, Dick? They can't take the loot with them."

"If they can't get it out using mules, how can we get it out with mules."

Perry scratched his head. "Yeah, Alf, explain that?"

"He can't," Pincham spit out.

"You bastards just eat, then we'll settle this whole mess."

Pincham laughed. "What mess? The one between us and them, Alf, or the one between you and me."

"Just shut up for a while."

Donner moved to his mule and grabbed the sack of supplies he had hooked over the saddle horn. He loosened the tie around the neck of the sack and poked his hand in. His fingers brushed against the sawed-off shotgun that freight line guards used. He was tempted to cock it and settle the dispute with Pincham and with Perry, if necessary. But the fact was, he might need them until he recovered the money. He extracted a handful of jerky and began to gnaw on the tough beef.

Pincham and Perry ate together. Donner thought he could hear them whispering. Pincham was right. Every man would have to watch out for his back, if he was going to survive this trip.

The cold and the snow dulled their tempers, but there remained an edge among them. Donner said nothing, just ate the tough beef. His mind was a numb as his fingers and his face. The misery, though, would be worth it once he had his fingers on that money.

Darkness came slowly and even when the glow of day faded from the clouds, Donner waited, testing the patience and nerves of his two questionable confederates.

"Are we going or not?" Pincham finally called.

"Thought you'd lost interest, Dick." Donner arose and carried his war bag to his mule. He hooked the supplies over the saddle horn and grabbed his rifle from under his saddle cinch.

"One of you stay here with the mules," Alf commanded.

"Nope," Pincham said, "we all three go. Who's to say you wouldn't try to kill that one and blame it on Blake Corley."

"My, my, you've become a suspicious one."

"Okay then, we all go together."

Pincham and Perry got their rifles and sidled toward Donner.

"Let's take it nice and quiet," Alf said. "The mules are hobbled, but we can lead them part way. At least until we hear signs of them."

Each man took the reins of his mount and began to advance as quietly as possible in the snow which crunched after their every footstep. They eased forward, their nerves as taut as a hangman's noose, suspicious of one another and uncertain of what awaited them down the road.

Occasionally they stopped to listen, but all they heard was the sound of their own breath and the shivering and blowing of the mules behind them.

Then Donner saw something in the middle of the road, maybe a barricade, and he could just make out the back of the wagon through the snow. But something was odd, something didn't seem right. Maybe they were walking into an ambush.

He lifted the rifle to his shoulder and fired a shot into the barricade.

Pincham growled under his breath an Perry flinched and the mules stamped, but the only thing else that answered the shot was the moan of the wind.

"They've pulled out," Donner announced.

"I told you, dammit," Pincham said.

Donner moved to the barricade and brushed the snow aside. He smiled to himself. It was the coffins, stacked one atop the other. "They left us a gift."

"The coffins?" Perry asked breathlessly.

"Before we get too excited we better make sure they're not sighting in on us right now and gonna shoot us," Pincham said, anger in his voice.

"You boys go ahead," Donner announced.

"Nope," said Pincham. "We advance together."

Donner grabbed a handle to the coffin and jerked on it. "The loot's still there."

"Now," said Pincham, "we'll check the rest of this out.

The three dropped the reins to their mules and slipped around the coffins, they made their way to the back of the wagon which was tilted precariously toward the cliff.

"I'll be damned," Donner said. "They sawed the wagon in half."

Pincham turned to Donner. "Alf, why would they've done that when they could just mounted the mules and rode away?"

"I don't know. . . ," Donner started then fell silent.

"Think about it, Alf."

Donner ran back to the coffin. He bashed the coffin lid with the butt of his rifle repeatedly, then stepped back and splintered the top until he could pry it open with the barrel of his gun. He shoved his hand inside and felt around.

It was filled with rocks.

"They got away, didn't they Alf? And, they got away with the loot."

Donner scowled. "They won't get away next time."

Sheriff Stewart Johnson was tired in the saddle when he heard the shot. He had had little more than a couple hours sleep since leaving Silverton on a dim trail that he suspected led to Alfred Donner and the stolen payrolls.

Along the way, Johnson had found a few signs—a discarded tin can, droppings from mules, and a couple shell casings at one location. That wasn't much, but it was more tangible than the hunch he had been following.

Johnson figured Alf Donner had planned the robbery, for he was the only one with the information on the money being carried in an inconspicuous freight wagon. Bibb Clack, Dick Pincham, and Luther Perry were involved in it, too, though Johnson suspected one of the three had died in the fire at the freight office.

The one man Johnson was uncertain of was Blake Corley. Johnson cursed himself for not checking the coffins when Corley pulled out of town, but the sheriff had seen the two dead men placed in those boxes and then seen them delivered to the freight company. Too, Corley's cabin on the Haney claim had burned down the day before he left town. Was that just coincidence or was it tied to the fire at the freight office?

A lawman learned to live with questions because they always exceeded answers. And, there were always men who thought they were smarter than the law. Maybe such men existed, but Johnson had never met one. It was his experience that every man doing wrong made a mistake—like the gunshot down the road.

Johnson pulled his rifle from his scabbard, then bent low and patted his bay on the neck. "Easy boy, don't panic."

Only fools would get out in such bad weather and try to make the trip to Durango. Johnson was probably the biggest fool of the bunch because he was following a hunch.

He thought he heard a thud, as if someone were hammering on a house. It was strange how the canyon and the snow and the distance could distort sound. Sometimes a man's eyes played a trick on him. Sometimes his ears. And, worst of all, sometimes his mind!

Then he thought he caught the sound of muffled voices. He reined up the bay, which blew and stamped.

For a moment, just the whisper of the cold answered. Then, heated voices carried through the snow. One sounded like Alfred Donner.

Johnson released the safety on his Winchester and shook the bay's reins. He leaned forward in his saddle, straining to see the men before they saw him. As he advanced, the voices became clearer.

"We ain't lost the loot yet, Dick," Donner called.

"Dammit, Alf, you've done everything you could to give it away," replied a voice that Johnson took to be Dick Pincham.

"Corley didn't know he was smuggling the loot out of Silverton. He never would've if you hadn't let Black Baldy see you hiding Pug's and Barney's bodies."

"Everybody's made mistakes but you, is that what you're saying, Alf?"

"I made one big mistake, Dick, and that was letting you and Luther and Bibb get involved. I was giving you a chance to have money for the first time in your lives. That was my mistake."

Pincham laughed. "You got us involved because you didn't have the guts to rob and kill."

The sheriff's bay whinnied. Johnson clenched his jaw, fearing Alf Donner or his men might have heard.

Then Johnson made out three dark forms, standing in the middle of the road. Two of them stood toe to toe. The third stood to their side, staring at what looked to be two empty coffins.

"This is the law," Johnson called. "Raise your hands."

They hesitated, standing in shocked silence, their dispute dying like their dreams of riches.

Johnson fired his carbine over their heads. "Do as I say," he commanded as he came upon them. Through the snow, he recognized Donner with Dick Pincham and Luther Perry. They raised their hands.

"Now, one at a time, lift your pistols from your belts and drop them. Any sudden moves, I'll kill you."

The men obeyed, but Johnson knew they were giving up too easy.

"Alf," Johnson started. "I see you've come back from the dead."

"Who was in your bed?"

"Bibb Clack," Dick Pincham answered.

"Damn shame, Alf, to kill one of your gang members."

"I don't have a gang, Stew."

"You did kill him, didn't you?" Luther Perry sputtered. "Dick was right about you."

"I might of fallen for it, Alf," Johnson said, "but you forgot to take his boots off. I didn't figure you'd sleep with boots on in a nice warm freight office, like that. What did you do, shoot him first or just knock him out?"

"I don't know what you're talking about, Stew."

"Sure you do. I'd put a little of it together, but you and

Dick filled in the rest with your argument. You thought you were smarter than the law, didn't you, Alf?"

He laughed. "Stew, you've still got to return us to Silverton. Fact is, you don't have anything on us. We don't have any of the money you're trying to recover. There's nothing you've said we can't deny and nothing you've said you can prove."

"We'll let a judge and jury decide that. I figure we can get all of you to hang."

"Hang?" Luther choked. "I didn't do nothing."

Johnson shook his head. "You killed Barney and Pug."

"Bibb Clack shot them both," Dick Pincham said.

Johnson shook his head. "It's true what they say about no honor among thieves."

"Stew, are you gonna sit here all day and jabber us to death or are you going to take us to jail?"

"Get on your mules." Johnson bit his lip. It would be a long, cold, and dangerous ride to Silverton. He had left in such a hurry that he had not brought any manacles.

"Our mules are hobbled," Pincham said.

"Then unhobble them."

All three men bent at once. Johnson fired in the air.

"Do it one at a time so I can watch and don't try for your rifles."

Alf laughed. "You got us now, Stew, but you won't have us long."

When it was his turn, Alfred Donner bent down to unhobble his mule. His lips turned into a sinister smile as he removed the rawhide straps and tossed them aside. As Donner straightened, his arm brushed against the canvas bag of supplies hanging from the saddle horn. He slid his hand along the canvas, getting a feel for the position of the sawed-off shotgun inside. It was barrel down. He licked his lips. Once he mounted, Donner knew he must turn his mule to shield the canvas bag from Sheriff Stewart Johnson.

The sheriff waved his rifle. "Mount up, one at a time. Starting with you, Pincham."

Donner stared at Johnson through the pelting snow. The snow would help him kill the sheriff.

Johnson shook his rifle at Luther Perry. "You next."

"I didn't do nothing to be hanged for," he pleaded. "Honest."

The sheriff shrugged. "Bad choice of company, Luther."

Perry grabbed hold of the saddle horn, shoved his foot in the stirrup, and pulled himself atop the mule.

Johnson swung the rifle over to Donner. "Your turn, Alf."

"What if I don't," Donner challenged, figuring to toy a bit with Johnson, perhaps make him hesitate when the showdown came.

"You'll die."

"Hell, Sheriff, I ain't froze yet and I've been out in this snow a good while."

"You won't have to worry about freezing because I'll shoot you."

"So you're judge and jury, too? Is that you?"

"Quit stalling, Alf."

Donner spat, confident he was galling Johnson's hide. "Once I'm in the saddle, Stew, you're as good as dead. You understand that?"

The rifle exploded and a bullet whizzed over Donner's head.

Instinctively, Donner grabbed his hat and ducked behind the mule. He grinned as the fingers of his left hand felt through the canvas supply bag and cocked one of the hidden shotgun's twin hammers.

"No more nonsense, Alf."

Donner lifted his head above the mule's back. "Don't shoot again. I'll mount up."

"Move."

Donner shoved his foot in the stirrup, grabbed the saddle horn, and slowly pulled himself atop the mule.

Johnson wagged the rifle barrel at the men. "Start for Silverton. I'll be behind you."

Donner pointed at the two empty coffins in the road. "Shouldn't you head for Durango, Stew? We ain't got the money. Blake Corley's got it. He hid it in the coffins. He's the one behind the robbery. We're just trying to recover the money for the company."

Johnson shook his head. "A crook wouldn't buy the Haney claim. I'll consider Corley honest until I find out otherwise. Now get moving."

Perry started his mule past the sheriff. Donner rattled the

reins on his mount and cut off Pincham, sliding in ahead of him and behind Perry.

"What the hell?" Pincham cried out.

"Just wanted to put a body between me and the sheriff's gun, Dick. Nothing personal."

"Sheriff," said Pincham, "you won't have to kill Alf, if you'll just let me do it. Let me kill him with my bare hands and I'll go to the gallows a happy man, the bastard."

"Shut up, all of you," Johnson ordered, turning his bay in behind them.

"It's a long ride back to Silverton," Donner reminded him, then laughed.

"Shut up."

Donner rode slumped in the saddle, glancing over his shoulder regularly to keep an eye on Johnson. He tried to steer his mule so Pincham and his mount were always between himself and the sheriff. He slid his left boot out from under the saddle, then slipped his foot under the canvas bag, trying to lift it. He thought better of it when he realized the barrel of the cocked shotgun rested on his boot. If the trigger snagged, it would blow his foot off. He gently lowered the bag and slipped his foot back in the stirrup. Slowly, he leaned forward over the mule's neck.

"What are you doing, Alf?" cried Johnson.

"I dropped my reins. Mind if I get them?"

"Hold on," Johnson said.

Donner clenched his jaw. Without looking he knew from the sound of the hooves crunching in the snow that Johnson was riding up to see for himself. Fighting his instinct to make his play at that moment, Donner froze.

Pincham, though, came to his aid, nudging his mule toward Johnson's horse as he passed.

"Watch it, Pincham."

Donner grabbed the canvas bag and slid it up in the saddle, balancing it between himself and the saddle horn. "I got the reins, Stew, and my war bag. I'm hungry."

"Hold up your hands."

Donner raised his arms.

"Higher."

Donner raised them the length of the reins. "That's as high as they'll go unless you want me to drop the reins again."

"Let your hands down easy and don't stick them in the war bag until I check it out."

Donner licked his lips and let his hands slide to his lap and the canvas bag. Slowly, steadily, he loosened the neck of the bag, making sure Pincham screened his hands from the sheriff's sight. He knew he could not pull the shotgun from the bag without being spotted so he would have to fire from the bag. His fingers worked their way inside the bag and down the stock, his index finger slipping inside the trigger guard as his thumb cocked the second hammer. He felt the second trigger go stiff beneath his finger.

Donner took several deep breaths, trying to steady his nerves. He could barely hear the sound of the hooves crunching through the snow for the pounding of his own heart. He had two chances to get the sheriff. If he didn't, he knew he was a dead man. He bit his lip, then let out a deep breath. He glanced back over his shoulder, getting a bearing on Pincham and the sheriff.

Every time he looked, it seemed Johnson was using Pincham and his mule for a screen himself.

As softly as he could whisper, Alf called, "Dick."

No answer.

"Dick," he said again, a little louder.

"Huh?"

"On three get past me."

."What's going on you two?" called Johnson.

"One," whispered Donner.

"Shut up, you two."

"Two."

Not waiting, Pincham kicked his mule into a trot.

"Three."

Pincham's animal darted past.

Donner jerked his mule around and saw Johnson's rifle spit a finger of fire. The bullet pinged into rock wall behind him.

In the flash of gunfire, he saw Johnson's grim face. There was not an ounce of fear in it.

Donner's hand quivered as he lifted the shotgun with his right hand. With the supplies inside, the canvas bag was heavier than Donner had expected.

Johnson's horse kicked and jumped.

Donner released the reins and grabbed the shotgun barrel through the canvas sack.

Johnson squeezed off another shot that flew harmlessly overhead.

Donner aimed the barrel at Johnson.

The sheriff's horse reared on its hind legs.

Donner squeezed the first trigger and the bag convulsed in his hands, the flash from the muzzle lighting the end of the canvas.

Johnson dropped the rifle.

Donner knew he had hit the sheriff for sure.

Instead of falling from the saddle, Johnson slapped at his coat and jerked his pistol.

Cursing at the flaming bag at the end of his shotgun, Donner ducked low over the mule's neck as he saw the flash of Johnson's pistol muzzle.

Then Johnson's mount tumbled forward just as Donner squeezed off his second shot. The horse neighed madly, then collapsed on the side of the road.

"You bastard," screamed Johnson, then squeezed off another shot.

Donner shoved his hand in the bottom of the sack, trying to find the carton of shells.

Pincham raced by on his mule, then Luther.

Tins of food tumbled from the hole in the bag before

Donner's fingers grasped the carton of shells. He pulled the sack and carton to his chest as his terrified mule danced about.

Another of Johnson's shots went high.

Donner bent over and grabbed the reins, then kicked the mule in the flank, sending him running back down the trail after Pincham and Perry.

He wasn't certain if he hit Johnson, but it didn't matter. He knew the sheriff's horse was dead and that would give them the time to lose the sheriff.

Behind him Donner heard one other gunshot from Johnson, then silence. Donner slowed his mount, then realized why Pincham had raced ahead. Pincham was running back to the rock-filled coffins. That was where they had discarded their rifles and pistols.

"Damn you," Donner yelled, for Pincham was planning to kill him.

Donner jerked back the reins on the mule. The animal fought his savage pull for an instant, then stopped in its tracks. Donner grabbed the carton of shells, then shook the canvas bag free of his shotgun.

Hurriedly, he ripped the top off the carton and grabbed a handful of shells, shoving them in his pocket. He squeezed two more between his fingers, then tossed the remainder over the ledge. Quickly, he broke the shotgun open, shook the hulls free and replaced them with fresh shells. He slammed the barrel shut, then cocked the hammers, both triggers going taut against his finger.

"Damn you, Dick, now you're gonna die," he said as he kicked his mule into a trot.

It seemed forever and then but an instant before he reached the coffins. He made out one man sitting on his mule and the other scrambling in the snow, trying to find the guns they had discarded when Johnson had disarmed them.

Pincham, on his hands and knees, moved about like a mad man.

Donner rode up and reined his mule. "What's your hurry, Dick?"

Pincham looked up. "Bastard," he yelled, then shot up from the snow, a rifle in his hand. He swung it toward Donner.

Donner's fingers jerked against the twin triggers and the shotgun convulsed in his hands.

Pincham never made a sound except for his flesh giving way to the shotgun blast. He collapsed on the snow, a bloody heap.

Even though the shotgun was empty, Donner swung it around at Luther Perry. "You with me or you with him, Luther?"

"I'm with you, Alf."

Donner laughed. "Wise choice. Poor Dick just donated his share to us, Luther."

25

Sheriff Stewart Johnson fired a final shot at the escaping robbers, then cursed. His rearing bay had saved him from the first shotgun blast, then the gelding's fall forward had saved him from the second. From the ache in his left leg, Johnson knew he had been hit by a few pellets. In the fall with the horse, Johnson had failed to jump free of the bay and his left leg was pinned beneath the animal.

Before he tried to free himself, Johnson broke open his revolver and reloaded in case Donner and his men returned. Then he beat the snow with his hand, trying to find the rifle he had dropped. His fingers finally slapped against it. He jerked it to him. If the men did return, he wouldn't be caught helpless.

He took a deep breath, and tried to extract his leg, but it didn't budge. He fought against the carcass until he was out of breath and sweating profusely.

As he rested, he cursed himself for the fool he was letting Donner get the jump on him. He knew he had a daunting task before him. First, he had to free himself before he froze. Then he had to get to Silverton or Durango. He had to arrest Donner and his two cohorts. At the moment, that seemed about as likely as the temperature rising above freezing before dawn.

From down the road, Johnson heard the booming retort of the shotgun, echoing like thunder through the canyon. "I hope it was you that got killed, Donner," he cried, suspecting it was more likely Pincham or Perry.

Johnson lay motionless, listening for any sound that might indicate what Donner was doing, but he heard nothing more.

His leg was stiffening on him and he was growing cold, half buried in the snow. He jerked at his leg and the horse didn't budge. He shoved the butt of his rifle under the saddle and pushed up, gaining enough leverage to wiggle his leg. Pushing the rifle a bit further under the dead animal, he shoved against the barrel, then wriggled his left leg, moving it a couple inches. Taking a deep breath, he pushed with his remaining strength on the rifle and tugged his leg. Then, he bent his right leg and shoved his free boot against the saddle for more leverage. He pried the rifle butt against the ground. Pushing with his right leg and shoving against the rifle barrel, Johnson eased the weight on his leg and gradually pulled it from beneath the dead bay. He caught his breath.

"Finally," he said, though he knew still hadn't saved himself. If the leg was broken, he was as good as dead anyway.

The leg was numb. He rubbed it briskly with both hands, trying to massage the feeling back into the limb. He pulled up his pants leg to rub his flesh and his hands grew sticky with blood. Despite the wounds, his leg did not feel broken. That, at least, was a good sign. He pulled his pants leg back down, slipped his pistol in his holster, then picked up the rifle and tried to stand

"Easy, easy." He encouraged himself, getting to his knees, then using the rifle as a crutch. He wobbled for a moment, then took a step with his bad leg, almost falling. His foot no longer seemed like it was connected to his body. He staggered forward, taking one, two, three steps, then resting.

He had a choice, Durango or Silverton. Silverton might be closer, but Durango was downhill and Durango was where Donner was headed. He chose Durango and started marching. The feeling gradually returned to his leg, but with it came pain. He gritted his teeth against the sharp jabs where the pellets had embedded in his flesh. He fought the pain as he staggered down the road.

Eventually, he came to the two coffins. Now there was a body sprawled out across the ground. Even though the face and torso were a bloody pulp, Johnson knew that it had to be Pincham. The body of a mule was lay not twenty feet from the man's body.

The demise of Pincham meant one less killer he would have to deal with at the end of the trail. He spat on Pincham and started marching.

He kept moving, certain if he stopped he would freeze to death. Gradually the pain seemed less of a problem than the monotony. He made it to the bottom of the canyon road. Time began to run into distance and he could not keep up with how far he had walked, only that when dawn came he was on a flat trail and he slipped away into a grove of pines and leaned against a tree for rest. When he awoke, he was face-to-face with a mule with bloody forelegs and a harness on his shoulders.

Johnson smiled. He would get to Durango sooner than he had thought.

26

Blake Corley didn't know how much of a lead they had on Donner and his men, but he knew they had to stop sometime soon to feed Penny Heath and warm her up. He could hear her teeth chattering as the cart moved down the road. The snow had not let up and though it was an impediment, it might also be their savior, allowing them to pull off the trail into the trees that now skirted the road and the river. Hidden among the trees and obscured by the steady snowfall, they could build a fire.

"She's shivering bad, Mose. We need to stop for a bit, get some food and warmth in her. Let's head into the trees."

Moses jerked the reins on his mount and the team turned off the road and into the forest. He guided the team through the trees as far as he could, but it was like trying to thread a needle with twine.

"This is about as far as we can go," Moses said, "and still be able to get out.

Blake glanced back over his shoulder and saw they were barely fifty feet from the road. "It'll have to do."

Both men dismounted and moved to the cart, Blake standing

on the wagon tongue and reaching for Penny. She shivered uncontrollably. "See if you can get up. I'll help you out."

"I'mmmm c-c-co-cold."

Moses grabbed the ax and headed into the trees. Shortly, Blake could hear the sound of Moses chopping wood.

Penny managed to sit up, but the exertion sapped her and Blake reached over to help her. He caught her under the shoulders and pulled her over the top of the driver's box. The buffalo robe and the blanket fell away from her. He grabbed them as best he could, then carried her to a tree. Dropping the buffalo robe in the snow, he laid her atop it, then covered her with the blanket and wrapped the robe back over her.

Moses came back with an armload of wood and kicked out a spot in the snow. He dumped the wood and reached under his coat, pulling out his hunting knife. He offered the knife to Blake. "Make some shavings and start a fire for Missy. You got matches?"

Blake shook his head.

Without a word, Moses shoved his hand in his pocket and gave a tin of matches to Blake, then disappeared in the trees.

Blake grabbed a stick of wood and began to whittle the end until he had a pile of shavings. He stacked the wood atop the shavings and pulled out a match from the tin. He flicked the match to life on his thumbnail and touched it to the shavings. The yellow flame spread, then grew, engulfing the shavings and licking its way up the other wood. Soon, the fire took hold and Blake held his hands to the warmth.

After sticking Moses's knife under his gun belt, he moved to Penny and picked her up in the buffalo robe. She shivered against him as he moved her near the fire.

"It's gonna be okay, Penny. You'll get warm soon."

With his boot, he kicked away the snow gouging out a place for her on the ground. The heat was already melting a circle around the fire. Blake placed her near the fire and lifted the buffalo robe so she could feel the warmth. He rubbed her back and arms through her thick coat which extended to her knees. Then he massaged her calves and feet. Gradually, she stopped shivering.

Baldwin returned with the ax and another load of wood, dumping it beside the fire. He chopped down a couple nearby trees eight- or nine-feet-tall, then dragged them behind Penny and positioned them head against foot. He retreated to the cart, removed the tarp, and covered the trees with it. "That'll screen the fire from the road, in case the men come by. How's Missy doing?"

"She feels warmer."

"We're gonna make it."

"Unless this snow doesn't let up and we get snowed in."

"We'll have plenty of money to burn," Moses laughed. "I'll get some food." He retreated to the wagon and returned shortly with the sacks of supplies. "I've still got a couple cans of frozen peaches and there's some jerky and crackers in this other one."

Blake nodded. "I'll feed her crackers."

As Moses handed Blake the tin of crackers, he eyed the road. "You think they're close?"

Blake shrugged. "Probably, but surely our luck will change."

"Hope Missy gets better. She's had it worst of all. I wish we could keep the fire going all night, but I figure we should burn what wood we have, then let it burn down to coals. Less chance of us being spotted. If our friends pass, they'll smell the smoke anyway."

"How we gonna keep her warm?"

"We've got an extra buffalo robe. I figure you can sleep with her."

Blake couldn't hide his surprise at the suggestion, but Moses misinterpreted it.

"I didn't mean nothing by that."

Blake lifted his hand. "I didn't take it as anything untoward, Mose, just I hadn't thought about that."

"Maybe your body heat can help keep her warm."

"What about you?"

"One of us has got to stand guard. We can't let them slip up on us in the night."

"We can't afford for you to get worn out, Mose."

"We got to keep Missy warm. I sure shouldn't stay in the same buffalo robe with her, no sir."

"You're a good man, Mose."

"I'm a black man, Blake. That ain't always easy."

Blake nodded. "Neither is being a good man."

Moses pulled a can of peaches from his sack and placed it near the fire. "She might like some warm peaches, too."

Blake began to feed Penny crackers until Moses pitched him the tin of peaches.

"It should be thawed enough to start feeding Missy."

Taking the hunting knife from his belt, Blake sliced it open and lifted the top, then gave the knife back to Mose.

"One question before I slip down to the road, Blake. You think if we left the money for them that would get them off our tail?"

"Not a chance. We know too much."

Moses scratched his head, then rubbed his chin.

"What are you thinking, Mose?"

"Maybe staying behind, bushwhacking the three of them, maybe catching one of their mules and catching up with you."

"You're not staying, Mose, you're going with us."

"I wouldn't want that either," whispered Penny.

Both men turned her. She wore a frail smile.

"How much did you hear, Missy?"

"Some."

"We weren't going to take advantage of you, Missy, honest."

"I know."

Blake shoved his hand to his mouth, bit the fingers of his glove and pulled it off with his teeth. He stuck his finger in the peaches and pulled out a slice, moving it to Penny's mouth. "Here's supper. It ain't much."

She took a deep breath. "It's food."

Mose stood up and retreated to the wagon, fetching the second buffalo robe and tossing it to Blake. He grabbed his rifle, then moved back down toward the road.

"Just a minute," Blake said to Penny, then jumped up, snatched the extra robe, and chased after Moses. "You keep this, Mose. We'll make do."

Wordlessly, Mose took the buffalo robe and disappeared in the snow.

Blake returned and began to feed her more peaches. She ate them ravenously, then drank the syrup when Blake tipped the tin to her lips.

"Just what did you hear, Penny."

She reached out and touched his bare hand wrapped around the can. "You mean about you joining me beneath the blanket and keeping me warm?"

Blake felt his cheeks burn with embarrassment.

"I heard that and I heard what Mose said."

"You're not mad."

"I'm alive because of you two. How could I be mad?"

"Thinking we might take advantage of you out here."

"Men have been taking advantage of me for almost a year, Blake."

He hung his head in embarrassment.

"And, I've been taking advantage of them, to make some money."

Blake scooped up snow with the empty can and sat it near the fire to make water. When the snow melted, he gave her the tin, pleased that she drank it.

"Would you do something else for me?" Penny asked, her voice soft, as soft as her smile.

"Sure."

"Keep me warm when the fire burns down?"

Blake was awakened by the sound of someone approaching in the snow. He lifted Penny's arm from over his as he slid his hand to the revolver at his hip. Penny nuzzled against him as he began to lift the pistol.

"Morning," she whispered, reaching for his arm.

He shoved it aside, drawing a surprised gasp from her. "Someone's coming," he said.

"Blake, Missy," called Moses Baldwin. "It's time we started for Durango."

Blake relaxed and holstered his revolver. He felt Penny's hand pat his arm through his coat. He had never felt closer to a woman in all his life and yet his flesh had barely touched hers during the night.

Lifting the buffalo robe, Blake slid out, embarrassed that Moses might see him with her, even though he had done nothing wrong.

"It snowed more," Baldwin called. "I bet we've got another foot of snow now. It's gonna wear the mules out."

"Did you get any rest, Moses?" Blake stood up and stretched his arms, yawning.

"I dozed off on occasion."

"No sign of Donner?"

"Not a bit. Maybe the snow's slowed him down more than us. How'd you sleep, Missy."

"Warm," Penny answered. "Best night's sleep I've had in a couple years."

"You sound better." Baldwin tossed his buffalo robe in he back of the cart, then retrieved the tarp and tossed it in as well.

"I'm still weak, but better."

"We'll get you to a doctor when we get to Durango," Blake said. "Make sure everything is okay."

Penny smiled at Blake.

Baldwin pointed to the sky. "The storm's breaking and the clouds are clearing out. The sun'll be hard on the eyes today. Need to be careful or we'll go snow-blind." Moses pointed to the ashes of the fire. "Rub some of that soot around the bottom of your eyes, Blake. You, too, Missy. It'll help cut the glare."

Blake figured Moses's suggestion couldn't hurt, so he smeared soot below his eyes, then did the same for Penny. "What about you, Mose, aren't you gonna follow your own advice."

Moses shook his head and started laughing. "My cheeks generally are dark enough without rubbing soot on them."

Shaking his head, Blake shrugged. "Didn't think about that." He bent over the buffalo robe and threw it back, helping Penny to her feet. She was wobbly, but her eyes were brighter and her cheek had more color than he remembered from the day before.

"Missy, I believe you're gonna be back to yourself in another day or two."

"Thank you, Mose. I owe it to both of you."

Moses grinned.

"You know, Missy, only thing that'd make you a better looking woman was if you had some of that natural soot all over you like me. Then I'd keep you warm and Blake there could stand guard over the road."

Penny stepped awkwardly through the snow to Moses and threw her arms around him, leaning into his chest.

Moses stood motionless, his arms limp at his side, not knowing what to do.

"You can hug her, Mose."

Softly, he put his strong, powerful arms around her.

"Thank you for everything you've done, Mose."

He patted her back. "Don't thank me until we get you to Durango."

Blake picked up the buffalo robe and blanket Penny had left behind and carried it to the cart where his path converged with hers. He helped her up into the seat.

"Odd looking wagon," Penny announced. "I thought I was just delirious yesterday, but you did cut the wagon in half."

"It was Mose's idea."

Moses grinned, then grabbed the ax and returned it to the cart. "The mules are looking pretty poor. When we get a chance, we need to run them down to the river, let them water real good."

"You're in the lead, Mose. Whenever you find a spot, point them to water."

Moses climbed atop the near mule, while Blake marched around the cart and mounted the wheeler on the opposite side. Baldwin lowered his rifle to the crook of his arm, then glanced over his shoulder to see if everyone was ready. Then he nudged the animal forward and the mule team began to circle out of the trees and back toward the road where the snow was deeper.

The sun was beginning to break through the clouds and shafts of brilliant light poured through the holes in the sky, creating white glares that scalded the eyes.

Gradually, Moses maneuvered the cart to the road, then aimed for Durango. Going was slow in the deep snow.

Penny sat in the seat briefly, then grabbed the buffalo robe and sank into the driver's box.

The river ran alongside the road, wide and noisy. The riverbed was rock-lined with occasional patches of high ground

where a pine or other tree had taken root among the rocks.
Blake could see Moses evaluating places where they could
leave the road to water the mules.

"Maybe we'll have to unhook the team," Blake offered.

"We can ride a bit further," Moses answered.

Blake looked up the road. A half mile away, the road narrowed between a steep, boulder-studded slope on one side and
a giant pile of boulders which anchored the other side of the
road near the river. The boulders stood on a patch of earth
where a half dozen pine trees grew. Because of the steep slope
from the road to the river bank, it seemed unlikely they could
reach the water without unhooking the team, at least not until
they got past the slope and boulders.

"Why don't we just unharness them, Mose?"

Moses shrugged. "Maybe it's instinct, but I don't like the idea
of unhooking the mules in case we have to make a run for it."

"Won't be much of a run with snow this deep."

Blake started to say something, until he saw the mule's
ears flick forward. He grabbed the gun at his waist, then studied the road ahead.

He caught a sudden glint of metal from the steep mountain slope overhead.

Moses saw it, too, for he jerked the reins hard to the river
side just as a shot rang out from the cliff.

"Dammit," cried Moses. "They must've slipped by me in
the night."

The mule beneath Baldwin squealed as it was struck by a
bullet.

Blake fired at the glint and his bullet pinged off the rock.

Moses slapped his dying mule and aimed him for the edge
of the road.

The animals plunged down the steep white slope for the
river, but it was nothing but snow and the front pair of mules
disappeared, then the wheelers hit the mushy incline and fell
five feet to a flat patch of ground.

Penny screamed.

The cart bounced down the drop, knocking Blake off his mule, then careened toward a trio of trees near the base of the pile of boulders. Moses, still grasping the rifle, jumped from the mule as it crashed into the tree. The cart stopped at the base of the tree and Penny began to sob. Then she arose from the driver's box and look around, her eyes ringed with tears and fright.

"Blake, Blake, where are you?"

28

Moses Baldwin ran through the snow to the jumble of rocks and scrambled to a perch where he could answer the fire from the opposite slope. He looked over his shoulder and saw Penny looking wildly about, screaming for Blake. Hearing no answer, Moses glanced toward the river and the cart, its left wheel broken. Of the four mules one stood terrified, dipping and tossing its head, two were thrashing on the ground with broken legs and, the fourth, the one Baldwin had been riding, was dead from the bullet wound. Fortunately, the cart came to a stop at the foot of a thirty-foot pine tree and behind the pile of boulders, screening it from the assassins. Moses looked back down the road, seeking some sign of Blake, then fell between two boulders and scanned the slope across the road for the ambushers.

He caught a glint of metal and snapped a shot off from his rifle, the bullet pinging off the stones. His shot was answered by two and he ducked as the splat of the bullets sent chips of rock flying. He kept his head low, but heard other shots, directed somewhere else. He peeked up and saw puffs of smoke from the slope, then realized the gunfire was directed down the road.

Behind him Penny screamed. "Run, Blake, run."

Moses twisted around and saw Corley wading through the deep snow, trying to reach cover. The bullets kicked up puffs of the powder as he ran. Seeing Blake stumble, then plow head first into the snow, Moses jumped up, slammed the rifle butt to his shoulder and emptied the magazine into the slope.

Moses dove for cover, hitting hard as the bushwhackers turned their fire on him. Moses lifted his head for an instant, but long enough to see Blake, slogging through the snow before making the base of the rocks and cover.

"You okay, Blake?" he yelled, as he fished into his coat pocket and reloaded from his dwindling supply of bullets.

"Am now."

Moses glanced over his shoulder and saw Penny wading through the snow toward Blake.

"It's all my fault," Moses said. "I must've dozed off and they slipped past me while I slept."

"Shut up, Mose, we wouldn't have made it this far without you."

"Maybe so, but it don't matter how far we get if we don't get to Durango."

Another shot from the slope pinged into the rock over Moses's head, then rattled around the other boulders. Baldwin cursed and retreated to another location.

"You seen them?" Blake called.

"Just their smoke. Is Missy okay?"

"Scared and hungry, that's all."

Moses glanced over his shoulder at the cart and the dead or thrashing mules. "You ever ate mule, Missy?" He laughed as he retreated down the rocks to find Blake and Penny, huddled together, their backs against the rocks.

"No time for you two to be warming each other up," he joked, trying to keep their spirits up.

Moses pointed to the two crippled animals. "We're running out of ammunition, but I can't let those two mules suffer." He gave Blake his rifle, jerked his pistol from its holster, and marched to each animal, placed the gun in its ear and fired. He unhitched the surviving mule and moved it to a tree near the base of the rocks. Retreating to the wagon, he glanced toward the opposite slope, checking to make sure the cart's resting place was screened from the bushwhackers' perch across the road. It was. He walked back to Blake, shaking his head, uncertain what to do.

Blake stared at the cart and its smashed left wheel. "It's over, Mose, unless you can fly or swim."

Moses shoved his pistol in his holster and reached to reclaim his rifle. Then it struck him like a bolt of lightning. "That's it, Blake. You just figured out how we're getting out of here."

"Huh, what are you talking about? You can't fly and I can't swim, there not being much need for it in Kansas."

"It don't matter none."

"You take that rifle and climb up among the rocks." Moses dug the carton of shells out of his coat pocket and handed it to Blake with the rifle. "Fire a shot now and then just to make sure they know we're still watching. See if you can keep them from changing positions on us."

"What are you gonna do?"

"Chop a little firewood, cook us a little mule meat while you keep watch. If you get a clean shot at one of their mounts, kill it and we'll see if we can put them afoot like they've done us."

Blake shrugged and turned to Penny. "You stay here and if Mose turns completely crazy, then you call me and I'll put him out of his misery."

Moses laughed. "Just trust old Mose. That's all you got to do, other than keep them from coming out of the hills to share our mule meat."

Penny shook her head. "Mule meat?"

"Missy, all we've had has been those frozen tins of peaches, some crackers, and some jerky. Granted this ain't no fine beef-steak I'm gonna be preparing, but it's meat. You want to butcher it?"

Vigorously she shook her head.

"That's okay, but once I get the fire going and some slabs of meat ready, I want you to cook them for me. Think you can do that."

"The fire'll keep me warm."

"Now you're talking." Mose turned to Blake. "Are you gonna get going and stand watch or hang around and tell Missy how to cook?"

Blake shook his head in exasperation. "I don't know what you're up to."

"And I'm not telling, other than I'm gonna have me a fine meal of roast mule meat and cut me a little wood. Now go along."

Blake climbed among the rocks, then started worming his way to a position to keep watch on the opposite slope.

Moses retreated to the wagon and got the ax and saw, then quickly chopped down a small tree and helped Penny build a fire. Then he took his hunting knife and skinned and sliced a shank of meat from one of the dead animals. He cut the meat in strips, poked it with sticks and carried it to Penny to cook.

Then, he picked up the ax and started chopping down the pine tree beside the damaged cart. He had a plan.

Blake Corley thought he saw movement on the slope across from him. He fired off a shot, then ducked behind rocks and moved to a new position so they would not shoot at the puff of his smoke.

Two shots from the slope answered his, but the smoke from their rifles had drifted away from the rifle muzzles before Blake could take up a new position.

Shortly, he caught the aroma of cooking meat and it smelled good, even if it was mule. He hoped the aroma reached Donner and his men and drove them crazy. Blake scanned the slope, straining to spot the bushwhackers, but he saw nothing and doubted he would see much for a while. The sun was beginning to singe wide holes in the clouds and to create a blinding glare. Fortunately, the sun was behind him and Blake figured it was easier for him to see than for his enemies.

Behind him, he heard the thud of an ax in a tree. Glancing around, he was blinded by the glare for a moment. He squinted his eyes tighter and made out Moses at the base of the thirty-foot pine tree by the cart. With each ax swing, Moses sent chips flying from the trunk. Blake couldn't understand why Moses, with assassins overhead, was actually chopping a tree down.

Blake shrugged. "That'll make a hell of a fire, Mose." Blake fought the glare to spy Donner and his men. He closed his eyes often to shut out the reflected light. At the sound of a noise below him, he looked around and saw Penny climbing through the rocks, carrying a piece of meat on the end of a stick.

"Keep low," he called to her as she approached. "You should be resting."

She smiled as she reached him. "You and Mose have done so much for me." He took the meat from her and began to eat it. Though tough, it was warm and it sat well on his stomach. "Don't tire yourself," he cautioned, then turned back to watch the slope as best he could through the glare.

"I'm better."

"Good." Blake didn't say anything else because he didn't know what to say. He couldn't promise her they would get to Durango. He couldn't express how sorry he was that she lost her child. Nor could he tell her how fond he had grown of her. Sometimes a man can find his lucky break at the end of a mine shaft, sometimes behind a poker hand, and, on occasion, in a woman. Though he didn't know what to say, he was comfortable with Penny nearby.

For a long time there was nothing but the silence between them, the roar of the river and the thud of Moses's ax blade in the pine tree below. Then the tree cracked and snapped. Through the haze of the glare, Blake saw Moses run from the tree as it crashed to the ground, throwing up a cloud of snow.

"Do you know what Mose is up to?"

Penny shrugged. "Wish I did."

"I guess he's making do like he did in the war."

At the retort of a shot from the slope, Blake motioned for Penny to stay down behind the rocks.

"Blake Corley," called a cry from the slope. Blake recognized Alfred Donner's voice.

"Let's talk, Corley."

"We don't have anything to talk about."

"Sure we do. You're carrying a fortune that belongs to me."

"I thought it belonged to the freight company."

"I've figured we could cut you in, give you a share. There's enough to go around."

"How much is there?"

"Hundred thousand dollars."

Blake whistled.

"What do you say, Corley?"

"I don't see any point in sharing it? You'd just kill us once we came out in the open. I'll sell you the Haney claim for it."

"You bastard. This is your last chance, Corley, for you and for that whore and nigger."

Blake jumped up from the rock, firing once, twice, three times before he heard Penny scream. She lunged for him, grabbing him around the legs and pulling him down, just as a half dozen bullets from above splattered their stony den, spraying them with chips of rock.

Penny moaned.

Blake feared she had been hit. He pulled her back behind a bigger rock, then turned her over. She grabbed at her face and he saw a drop of blood where a bit of rock had nicked her.

"He was just trying to rile you, Blake, get you to do something foolish like stand up so he could shoot you."

"He called you a whore and Mose a nigger."

"He's a desperate man."

Blake pulled her to him, pressing her cut cheek to his coat. "We'll get out of here sometime and when we do, I'll never let another man call you a whore."

"I'm not a school marm, Blake."

He patted her head beneath the shawl that covered her yellow hair. "We'd best move to a new position, keep him guessing like Mose is keeping me guessing."

"I need to get back to the fire. Mose said he wouldn't eat until he downed that tree. I'd best go cook his meat."

Blake kissed the shawl. "Keep low."

Penny pulled herself away and retreated. Blake watched her until she moved out of sight, then he slipped to a new position between a couple boulders where he could hide in the deep shadows and screen his eyes from the blinding glare of the climbing sun.

"Corley," Donner called again.

"Go to hell."

During the silence that fell between them, Blake tried to figure a way out of their predicament. Then he heard the hoarse sound of a saw biting into timber. Looking down from his den, he saw Moses sawing a ten-foot length of the pine tree he had just downed.

What the hell was Moses doing?

30

When he saw Penny return to the fire, Moses Baldwin made a couple more drags on the saw, then moved toward her.

Penny picked up a stick of meat and held it over the flame. The searing meat sizzled and the aroma made his empty stomach churn.

"What happened to your cheek, Missy?"

Penny touched her cheekbone. "A bit of rock stung me from one of their shots at Blake." She handed him the stick of meat.

He bit into the meat.

"Blake stood up to shoot at them because they called me a whore."

"I thought it was because they called me a nigger." Moses grinned sheepishly when Penny stared at him. He shook the stick at her. "You're a good cook, Missy, even for mule meat."

Penny turned toward the downed tree and pointed at the saw embedded in it. "Blake can't figure out what you're doing."

"Making do, Missy, making do."

"Why won't you tell us?"

"I'm not sure it'll work and if it don't, I'll be the only one to know."

"You think we'll get out of here, Mose?"

"Sometimes if you ask yourself too many questions, you give yourself a reason to fail, Missy. Just trust me."

"I already have, Mose. There's no two men alive I trust more than you and Blake."

Moses stood up. "I best get back to work so we won't have to spend the night here." He wiped his mouth with the back of his hand, then moved to his saw and began to cut through the log. After completing the cut, he moved up the pine tree, stepping off ten feet and began another cut with the saw. It was slow work because he was tiring, but it was their only hope. Durango could be reached by road or Durango could be reached by water. With all the snow, the road was slow travel, but the water, it could carry a man there fast, if he had a boat or a raft.

By Moses's calculation, he could cut two sections of log about ten to twelve feet each, then remove the remainder of the wagon box from the undercarriage and attach the wagon box to the two logs which would give it enough buoyancy for all three of them and their supplies to make it to Durango.

With only one surviving mule, the raft was their only chance.

When he finished sawing the second log, Baldwin carried the saw to the cart and put it in the back. He removed the chain from the driver's box and the undercarriage and used it to wrap around one of the logs. He unhooked the mule and used the chain and animal to drag the log back to the wagon box. Then he maneuvered the second log to the opposite side of the cart and positioned it there.

He took the mule back beneath the rocks and tied him until he needed the animal to drag the raft into the water.

As he walked back to the wagon box, he saw Penny standing on her feet and smiling.

"A raft, isn't it?"

"Just making do, Missy."

Baldwin unloaded the wagon box, removing the four strongboxes, then the sacks of supplies, Penny's valise, the tarp, the buffalo robes and remaining blankets, the tools, the can of bolts and nails, and the leather lines that had been the wagon reins before Blake had shortened them to make reins for each mule.

Baldwin looked beneath the wagon's smashed wheel and saw that that side of the undercarriage had been sheared loose when the cart ran off the slope. He scooted around to the other side where he wasn't so lucky. The bolts had held. He could chop through the wood frame with the ax but might damage the wagon box. He kicked at the snow and went to the tools, then dug around in the can of nuts and bolts, finding a pair of pliers.

Taking the pliers he attacked the nuts and was finally able to loosen and remove them from the rusted bolts. He shoved the nuts and pliers in his pocket, then pulled the wagon box off the undercarriage. It fell in the snow.

Marching around the wagon box, he dragged the undercarriage away, then rolled the logs closer to the wooden box. He lifted a side of the wagon box and wrestled it over the adjacent log. Circling the raft, he lifted the other side of the wagon box and rolled the log beneath it. Taking the nails and hammer, he nailed the plank wagon bed to the logs, then nailed straps of the leather lines to the logs and ran them through holes in the floor before, wrapping them around the logs and nailing them again to the logs. He spent more than an hour securing the wooden box to the logs, then nailed and strapped a crosspiece at the front and the back of the logs, trying to give the raft more strength. There was only so much he could do with limited materials and that was about it. He salvaged the wagon tongue, then ripped up the plank used for the seat and nailed it to the end of the wagon tongue. It wasn't much of a rudder, but it was the best they could do. He propped the tongue over the top of the wagon box, then rested it on the cross piece where he used more leather straps to secure it.

He ignored a couple gunshots from up high and began to reload the wagon. He piled everything in except the ax, then he took it and chopped the front of each log to a point so the heavy logs wouldn't dig into the ground when the mule pulled it into the water. He hooked the chain to one of the logs, then drove the mule to the raft and linked the chain to the harness.

"Missy," he called, "come get in." Then he yelled at Blake.

When Blake glanced his way, Moses motioned for him to retreat from the rocks. Blake fired a final shot, then scrambled away from his hiding place. Moses swatted the mule on the flank and urged the animal toward the water. For an instant, the weakened mule seemed unable to budge the raft.

"Hiya," Moses yelled, and the raft began to slide toward the river. Moses ran behind and pushed against the log, just as Blake ran up, handed Penny the rifle and threw his shoulder against the raft. When the raft hit the water, Blake grabbed the wagon box.

"What if this thing don't float, Mose. I can't swim."

"Do what I always do," Moses answered. "Close your eyes."

31

The noises concerned him. Alfred Donner squinted against the glare, but could see nothing. What could Corley and Black Baldy be doing? Donner knew he had hit the lead mule when he shot at the black man, but he was uncertain how many of the remaining mules were fit to ride. He figured at least one and possibly two more were injured. If they had only one mule left, it couldn't carry all three of them, but if they had two mules, they could make a run. If they did, Donner knew they would try to circle behind the rocks that hid them and hit the road ahead of him and Luther Perry.

"Luther," Donner called. When Luther glanced up from his position, Donner motioned for him to come over.

Perry ducked between the rocks and made his way over to Donner. "What do you think, Alf?"

"Been a lot of hammering and sawing. Maybe they're trying to repair their cart. It hit hard when they ran off the road."

Perry nodded. "It's a shame the cart came to a stop out of our sight. Why do you think they cut that tree down?"

Donner shrugged. "They've got to make a run for Durango

so I want you to slip down to the road and set up there in case they try to get around us."

Perry cocked his head, stroked his chin, and eyed Donner with doubt.

"What you waiting on, Luther?"

"This ain't a trick, is it, Alf? You ain't gonna take the mules and leave me here to freeze or go blind, are you? You aren't gonna kill me like you killed Dick, are you?"

"Dammit, Luther," Alf said, offering Perry his rifle, "take this if you think I'm gonna shoot you. Take the mules if you think I'll run out on you. Only thing you're not taking when we finish this is my share of the money. Do you still want to be rich?"

Perry nodded. "That's why I've stuck with you, Alf."

"Corley has our fortune, Luther. If he gets away, neither of us'll be rich. Work your way down by foot, it'll be easier than trying to take your mule. If they make a run past you, I'll bring our mules down, then we'll ride after them."

"Okay," Perry replied, turning and starting back to his perch, before disappearing among the rocks.

Donner grinned. He'd take Luther for the ride as long as he could use him, then he would kill him and take his share of the loot as well. However, he might not have to kill Luther, as slow as he was. If Corley and the others made a run for it on their surviving mules, they wouldn't be able to carry much of the loot. If they did make a break, Donner would claim his mule turned up lame and send Perry to catch them. While Perry gave chase and perhaps got killed on his own accord, Donner would recover the loot.

Then panic set in. What if the noises he had heard had been them hiding the take somewhere? He might never find the money. In anger, he squeezed off a shot at the rocks across the road. "Damn you."

He took no comfort in hearing their occasional shouts to one another. They were probably spending more time hiding the money. Donner tried to spot them but the glare was bad and his eyes were aching. He did glance down the road to see

Luther taking position in a favorable spot that would put him in easy range of the three if they tried to escape. Donner wished he had told Luther to kill their mules if he couldn't hit them. At least that way, they would be afoot. But, he hadn't told Perry that and Perry was too dumb to figure it out on his own.

Donner settled into the shade and closed his eyes, listening for clues and trying to save his sight for when the three made their escape try. Across the road, he heard Black Baldy call to Blake. A gunshot followed and Donner heard the thud of a bullet thirty feet up slope.

Squinting, Donner lifted his rifle, rested the barrel on a rock and looked for the puff of smoke to aim at. He saw nothing, but he heard the sounds of men grunting and doing heavy work. What was going on? He studied the rocks as best he could in the glare, then noticed a movement in the water.

"Dammit," he cried. They had built a raft from what was left of their cart. That was what all the noise had been about. He jumped atop the boulder, almost slipping and falling from its icy surface, then jerked his Winchester to his shoulder and began to fire away at the raft. His eyes were so bad he could not see where the bullets were hitting, though one sounded like it hit wood. The others, though, plopped in the water.

"Luther," he screamed. "They've built a raft. They're floating away, dammit."

Perry emerged from his hiding spot.

"What?" he yelled.

"They've built a raft. They're on the water." If Luther didn't understand immediately, the raft would be past him. Donner pointed to the river and the raft. "They're escaping, dammit, on the water."

Seeming to catch on, Perry spun around and spotted the raft, then twisted back as if confirming that Donner had been right.

Donner cursed as Perry finally lifted his rifle to his shoulder and fired rapid shots at the raft. Though he was much closer, Perry missed, then dodged return shots from Blake Corley.

Donner jumped from the boulder and scrambled for the mules, untying them, mounting his and backtracking to the trail, then riding as quickly as he could down to the road and then through the thick snow to Perry. He tossed Perry the reins. "We've got to ride."

Before Perry could mount up, Donner pushed his mule ahead, but no matter how fast he could made the mule go against the snow, it wasn't fast enough. The raft gradually pulled away from him and then floated around a bend and out of sight.

Donner reined up and just stared. He had never seen a fortune float away before.

When Perry caught up with him, he gasped. "Where are they?"

"They're gone, Luther. It's no use chasing them."

"Does that mean the money's gone?"

"Maybe, though I do have a friend in Durango."

32

The raft bucked with the rushing current, tossing spray in their faces as they left the bushwhackers behind. Despite the cold, they smiled, congratulating one another on outwitting Donner and his men.

"I just saw two chasing us on the road," Blake Corley noted.

Moses Baldwin manned the rudder, moving it back and forth, trying to keep the raft in the deeper part of the river, rather than letting it drift into the rocks that lined the banks.

"Mose," said Blake, "nobody's better than you at making do."

Penny affirmed Blake's judgment. "We'd a been dead a couple times by now if it hadn't been for you."

Moses shoved the rudder hard to the right and the raft eased past a rock just peeking above the rippled surface. "I'd a been dead if you two hadn't given me a ride."

Penny wiped spray from her face, but Blake thought she might be hiding a tear as well. "Desperation drove us together, but what'll we do once we get to Durango?"

Moses toed a strongbox. "Spend our money."

Blake stared hard at Moses.

Moses glared back, then broke out laughing. "I was just joshing you, Blake."

"What are we going to do with the money?" Penny asked. "Where'll we take it?"

"Sheriff's office," Blake said, matter-of-factly.

Moses shrugged. "The sheriff's office is in the middle of town. The freight office sits on the river and we won't have to carry the strongboxes as far. The freight office can handle it from there."

"How far you reckon we are from Durango?" Penny asked.

"Twenty miles, Missy."

"Seems like we've been traveling long enough to get to California by now." She pulled her coat tighter around her.

"Snow—and those mean men—slowed us down, Missy."

"Let's go as far as we can before dark," Blake said.

"No way I want to ride this river in the dark," Moses agreed. He nodded, squinting as he steered the raft between the boulders scattered like giant marbles in the rushing water.

The splashing waters soaked them as they floated toward Durango, but the afternoon sun help keep them warm. When the sun dropped behind the mountains, Penny started shivering, her teeth clattering.

Blake eased to her side, pulling her close to him and shielding her from the splashing waters. "Penny's got the shakes awfully bad, Mose. Maybe we ought to make camp and a fire."

"Let's go a little farther, Blake."

"It's hard on her, Mose."

Moses waved away Blake's protest. "I remember a prospector's cabin abandoned a mile or so downstream. It'd be nice to have a roof over our head."

Blake stared along the road for the cabin.

"You're looking on the wrong side, Blake. That's the nice thing about this cabin. It's across the river. Donner'll have to get wet to get to us."

They rode the river for another half hour before Moses

pointed to a copse of trees. Blake stared for a moment, then just made out the shape of a snow-covered cabin.

The river was wide by the cabin and the current steady but not so powerful that Moses couldn't steer the raft into the bank forty feet from the cabin itself.

Moses studied the bank, then shook his head. "It's no good here. There's nothing we can tie on to and no place to hide the raft."

He let the current pull the raft away from the bank, then he steered farther downstream to a calm inlet behind a huge boulder which had tumbled down from the mountain centuries ago. Though more than a hundred feet farther from the cabin than the first landing site, a couple pine trees provided a solid place to tie the raft.

"It's a longer walk," Moses said, "but if Donner should travel the night and pass us, less likely he would see the raft tied here."

"You think of everything, don't you Mose?"

"It's called making do." Moses sat the rudder, then climbed out of the wagon box on one of the log pontoons, and jumped onto the bank. He used the chain to hook the raft to one of the trees. "I'll cut some small trees and bring them down here to cover the raft so it won't be as noticeable." He stepped back on the log, his arms outstretched. "Hand me Missy."

Blake swept her off her feet and passed her to Baldwin. He took her in his strong arms and jumped for the bank, agile as a deer.

"I'll get her inside. You bring what food and bedding you can, but leave the ax. I'll chop us plenty of wood."

Blake stood watching as Moses trotted the fifty yards to the cabin without missing a stride. He wondered where Moses got such endurance. Blake gathered the supply sacks and then the blankets. He crawled over the sideboard and jumped for the bank. Blake ran up the slope toward the cabin, tiring from the slight load he was carrying.

At the dwelling, he saw that the door had fallen from its leather hinge and that some of the chinking was missing between the logs. Even so, this cabin was the welcomest shelter he had ever seen. Inside, the windowless cabin was dark. Moses sat Penny on a stool and let her rest her back against the wall. A wood bed frame with rope webbing but no mattress stood on its end against the wall opposite the chimney. There was a washtub and a pail by the chimney as well as some empty tins scattered about the floor.

"Missy's shivering bad. I'll go chop some wood so we can get a fire going. You get the buffalo robes and fix her a bed." Moses disappeared out the door.

Blake draped one of the damp blankets over her shoulder. "I'll be back in a moment, Penny."

She moaned.

Blake ran down to the raft and gathered the two buffalo robes and her valise. Moses had already taken the ax and the rifle into the trees.

Back in the cabin, Blake pulled down the bed frame and moved it beside the dark chimney, then draped a buffalo robe over the rope webbing. Stepping to Penny, he helped her up and guided her to the bed, putting her down on the open robe, then closing it over her. "Mose will be back with wood for a fire, then you'll be warm."

She nodded. "I'm just cold and tired. It's nothing like it was last time."

Moses returned with an armload of wood and dumped it in front of the fireplace. "You'll be warm in a minute, Missy." He tuned to Blake. "You still got your tin of matches?"

Blake patted his pocket and nodded.

"Good. Start us a fire. If you hear a gunshot, don't worry I saw a deer in the woods. If I can get him, we'll have fresh meat."

Moses disappeared out the door again. For light, Blake left the door open long enough to build the fire, then he propped it shut. Gradually the room began to warm. Mose returned, kicked open the door and dumped another load of wood inside. "I'm gonna chop me a good size tree down and drag in as big a log as I can. You stay here and keep an eye on Missy."

Once again, Moses retreated before Blake could answer. In another ten minutes, a gunshot punctuated the air.

Penny flinched, then rose from her bed. "That's not them again is it?"

"It's Mose shooting us some meat."

"I hope it's not mule again."

Blake laughed. "Likely venison." He kept feeding the fire and the cabin grew comfortable. He pulled off his coat and placed it on the floor to dry in front of the fire. Penny asked for help removing her coat and Blake assisted.

"I've a clean dress in my valise, if you'd get it for me."

Blake carried her bag to the side of the bed by the fire and opened it up. The first thing he saw was Penny's Bible. "A Bible," he said. "I didn't know that . . ." he stopped when he realized what he was about to say.

"You didn't realize whores read the Bible?"

Blake grimaced and lowered his head. "I didn't mean nothing by it. I'm sorry, Penny." He looked at her but she turned away. He feared he saw a tear.

He didn't know what else to say, but she saved him the effort.

"After all you've done for me, treating me like the lady I'm not, I shouldn't have jumped you. That life is past now. I'm looking toward the future from now on."

33

Sheriff Stewart Johnson had grown accustomed to the pain in his leg, but riding the damned mule bareback had put a crease in his tailbone that seemed to ache like it was on fire. To break the monotony, to ease the pain, and to mask his hunger, he had taken to talking to himself. He doubted he would ever catch up with Alfred Donner and he mentioned that bastard frequently.

It was nearing dusk when the road up ahead went between a steep rocky slope on one side and a huge rock pile on the river side. As he neared, he saw tracks in the snow where a wagon—or what was left of a wagon—had run off the road.

He aimed his mule down the wagon tracks and the steep shoulder that led to the water. Near the water, he saw a smashed wagon wheel and part of a wagon undercarriage. Then he noticed the three dead mules.

"What the hell?"

Dismounting, he limped among the debris and the mule carcasses, still uncertain what had happened. He saw tracks made by men in the snow and a particularly deep set of twin ruts which led to the edge of the water. He examined the carcasses and found one which had had strips of flesh carved from its side.

Retreating to the rocks, he saw the cold ashes of a dead fire and, on a rock by the ashes, spotted two strips of roasted meat on a stick. Picking up the stick, he ate the meat, even though it was cold as ice. The mule flesh felt good on his stomach.

As he gnawed on the meat, Johnson limped back to the edge of the river and studied the sign. Then he laughed.

"You smart sons of bitches. You made a raft, didn't you? Good for you, dammit. Make Alf Donner work for his stolen money. You saw a wagon in half, then make a raft out of what's left. Good for you," he yelled.

His mule never flinched at his shout, too tired and too frozen to startle or even wander to water's edge for a drink.

Johnson went to the river, squatted down on his hands and knees and scooped water to his lips to wash down the roasted meat.

When he was done, he led the mule to river for water, then climbed atop the mule and continued his freezing journey toward Durango.

He wondered if Blake Corley would keep the money. Money had a way of changing weak men. Alf Donner was a weak man, but Johnson couldn't say about Corley.

The road ahead seemed endless. He rode with head and shoulders slumped. He was so tired that he dozed off as he rode, but he didn't stop because if he did, he might never wake up, freezing to death in the bitter cold. If he didn't get to Durango, he would never have a chance at catching Alfred Donner.

"Bastard," he said to the trees as he passed.

When darkness finally smothered out the last light of day, Johnson rode on. He would not quit riding until he found Donner and Donner would not quite riding until he had found the money.

Unless Blake Corley was a crook and kept the money for himself, Johnson told himself that search would end soon.

And, it would end in Durango.

If only Johnson made it there.

34

Well after dawn, when shards of sunlight slipped through the holes in the chinking, Blake Corley awoke first. The fire in the fireplace had turned to glowing embers and the cabin was cool, though not nearly as cold as the previous nights they had spent on the trail. Moses Baldwin snored heavily, as well he should have for all the work he had done. Occasionally between Moses's snorts, Blake could hear the soft fall of Penny's breath. He felt as low as a man could get for his unfinished comment on her Bible reading, but didn't know how to make amends. An apology didn't seem enough.

Blake slipped from his buffalo robe on the ground to the fireplace and added more of the wood Moses had chopped. Scattered among the embers were bones from the deer Moses had killed for their supper. Flames from the embers began to lick the fresh wood and the fire began to crackle and pop, sending sparks flying.

He slipped back to his bedding and crawled beneath the blanket and the top of the buffalo robe. He twisted to watch Penny, or at least that third of her face he could see beneath her buffalo robe and blanket. She was a fine looking woman

168

with a good heart and a decent spirit. He hadn't thought about it until she had raised the question the day before, but what would happen once they reached Durango? In a few short days Penny Heath and Moses Baldwin had become such a part of his life that it seemed they had been friends since childhood. What would they do after they reached Durango and returned the stolen money?

As his mind wandered, he realized he was being watched. He focused on Penny again and saw her blue eyes staring him.

She smiled. "Good morning."

He nodded.

Penny yawned. "I slept well and warm." She nodded toward Moses. "Sounds like he's still sleeping well."

"Mose has worked hard and kept us alive, or at least a step ahead of Donner."

Penny sighed and pulled the buffalo robe tighter around her neck. "I don't want to go out in the cold again."

"I reckon Durango could wait a day. I have to admit I could use more rest and the way Mose is snoring, I know he needs it. We'll talk it over with him when he wakes up."

She pointed to the washtub and pail in the corner. "We could even bathe and wash our clothes. I'd sure like to get the soot off my face before I get to Durango."

"You may have some extra clothes to wear, but I don't. What I had left burned down in my cabin before I left."

"You could wrap in a blanket. "It's not like I haven't seen a man naked before."

Blake sighed. "About my comment last night, I . . . "

Penny slipped her hand from beneath the blanket and shook her finger to chide him. "I said last night I was only looking to the future, not the past. You forget that and I will too."

Moses grumbled and shook himself awake. He stretched, yawned widely and arose suddenly from between his blankets, the fire casting a giant shadow of him on the wall. He had a wild look about him.

Blake stared, shaking his head.

"What's a matter with you?" Moses asked.

"First time I've seen you get up in the morning, Mose. Did anyone ever tell you you were damn ugly."

Moses cocked his head and eyed Blake. "Nobody's ever told me that."

"I didn't think so, Mose, and I can't understand why Penny'd have me inform you of that."

"Blake," Penny gasped, then swatted at him with her hand, "I didn't say no such thing."

"Missy, don't you worry none. I know you wouldn't say something like that."

Blake cackled until Moses wagged a finger at his nose.

"Least I wasn't scared on the raft, Blake. Yesterday on the raft I never saw you but that your eyes weren't closed, like you was praying." Moses laughed and Penny with him.

"I was praying for help if I needed to swim."

"It's a lot like flying, Blake. Remember what you told me on the cliff road? Just start flapping your arms."

"I had more water in my coat when I shucked it last night than I'd ever seen in Kansas. And, I just now feel like I'm beginning to dry out."

Moses shrugged. "Don't get too dry. We've still got a half day or more to get to Durango."

"That's what Penny and I wanted to talk with you about."

Moses twisted around on his bedding and drew his knees under his chin. "You're taking my share of the money," he grinned.

"No, no," Blake answered. "We just figured we could stay an extra night here in the cabin. It's warm and the bedding is satisfactory. An extra day won't hurt us. What do you think?"

Scratching his chin, Moses shrugged. "We could use the rest and I'd like to feel warm for a bit. Only thing is, Donner could beat us to Durango."

Blake held up his hands. "I don't figure we'll have to worry about Donner once we get to Durango and turn over the money."

"Donner's the type of man you've always got to worry about."

Penny interrupted. "Let's stay one more night, Mose. I'd like to take a bath, even wash my clothes, rest a little more. You could take baths, too."

Moses grinned. "You two look plenty dirty, wearing soot under your eyes and all, so you sure need a bath. Dirt don't show on us black folks."

Blake grabbed his hat and flung it at Moses, who fell back on his bed laughing.

"Sure, let's stay. We've more venison hanging outside and I'll chop us more wood so we can stay plenty warm. I guess I can tote water from the river up here for you to bathe."

"No, sir," Blake said. "You've done all the wood chopping up to now. I'll do it."

"I didn't know you Kansas sodbusters knew how to chop wood, seeing as how there was nothing to practice on in Kansas." Moses laughed.

"I guess we're all feeling better," Penny said.

Blake and Moses pulled on their boots, then climbed to their feet. Moses tossed Blake his hat then picked up his own. They stepped to the fireplace and backed toward the flame, the heat seeping quickly through their clothes and warming their flesh.

Moses stepped away from the fire first, slipping into his coat and grabbing the ax by the door. "I'll chop the wood and you haul the water." Moses was out the door before Blake could argue.

Blake grabbed his coat from the floor, shoved his arms in it and buttoned it up. He took the pail from the corner and headed outside, propping the door shut as he left. He clung to the trees to screen his approach to the river so Donner or any passing rider might not see him.

At the river, he filled he bucket and started back to the cabin, where he found Penny had moved the washtub near the fire. "This'll help warm the water up some."

It was a slow process. Blake making six trips to the river to fill the wash tub enough for a reasonable bath. Then the water took a long time to warm. When the water was warm, though not hot, Blake helped Penny ease the tub from the fire and then left her alone to bathe.

Baldwin brought several loads of wood and finally dragged a nine-foot freshly-cut log to the door. "We'll slide this inside and saw it in pieces under a roof instead of in the cold. He looked perplexed that Blake didn't offer to open the door. He dropped the log and moved to open it himself."

"Penny's bathing,"

"Ooops," he said. "Reckon I'll check the raft and everything there, see if it's still well hidden. And one other thing."

"Yeah?"

"No peeking!" Moses grinned.

"I've thought about it."

"Me, too."

"I heard that," came Penny's voice from inside.

Blake felt his face flush. Moses just laughed then retreated to the river.

Fifteen minutes later, Penny called for Blake to enter. he opened the door and smiled. She was standing there in a clean, dark blue dress, combing her wet hair. She was pretty as a picture.

"You ought to use the water and go ahead and take a bath."

He hesitated.

"Don't worry, I've seen naked men before."

"Not this one, you haven't," he answered.

"I won't peek. In fact, I won't even think about it." She giggled.

Blake began to undress and when he got down to his long underwear, Penny, turned around long enough for him to step out of his drawers and sit in the tub, his arms and legs hanging out.

"Is it safe to turn around?"

"Safe as it'll ever get," he said, starting to splash water upon his chest.

She marched by, picking up the dirty dress she had been wearing and throwing it in the flames.

"Why'd you do that?"

"Too many bad memories in that dress, Buford's attack, losing the baby, those things."

"It was the dress I met you in."

Penny walked behind him and kissed him on the top of his head, then retreated to the bed.

When he was done, Penny gave him a blanket to dry with. He wrapped himself in the blanket and sat in front of the fire.

Blake heard Moses approach, then rap on the door. "Okay to come in?"

"Yeah," Blake called.

Moses marched in, carrying another armload of wood.

"You're next," Penny said.

"There's more wood I need to bring in and the log to keep us through the night."

"You might want to dump the water, Mose, and fetch some more, six pails full," Blake said. "Since you black folks don't collect so much dirt, Penny can wash our clothes in that water after you're done."

Moses never complained, just brought in more firewood and finally dragged in the log. He made seven trips to the river for water, leaving the extra pail for drinking. Then, after making sure Penny wasn't looking, he stripped and sat down in the washtub.

He bathed quickly and when he was done, Penny dropped a buffalo robe to kneel on beside the washtub, then rolled up her sleeves and began to clean their clothes, draping them as she finished over the stack of firewood to dry.

Wrapped in the wool blankets, Blake and Moses sat by the fire, enjoying the warmth and the rest. Finally, their clothes dried, and they put them back on.

Baldwin went outside and carved off a chunk of deer meat. Penny cooked it over the fire. After eating, Blake took the saw and began to cut the log into lengths to fit the fireplace. When he finished, Moses would take the ax and split the wood.

When they were done, the men sat down with their backs against the wall and watched the fire. Penny joined them, carrying her valise and rearranging its contents.

She pulled out her Bible and a tintype.

Blake caught a glimpse of it. "Who's the woman?"

"My mother."

Blake took the tintype from her. "I see where you get your good looks."

For once, Blake thought he saw Penny blush.

"What's the book?" Moses asked.

"My Bible. Care to read it?"

Moses hesitated, seemingly uncertain what to say. "I can't read." He hung his head.

Without missing a beat, Penny smiled. "Lot of folks can't read."

They passed the afternoon in front of the fire, not saying much, just soaking up the warmth and enjoying the rest.

Before dusk, Moses grabbed his coat and hat and stepped outside. "I'll be back. I want to check on the raft."

He was gone thirty minutes. When he returned, he had a wide slab of venison in his hand and a frown on his face.

"What's the matter, Mose?"

"Donner. I spotted him and another man pass by on the road to Durango."

"Did he see you?"

"No, I'm sure he didn't."

"Then we've nothing to worry about. At least we know where he is and he doesn't know where we are."

Penny cooked the venison over the fire, then shared it and two of their remaining tins of food with the men. They tossed the bones in the fire when they were done and sat back and let the food settle.

"Missy, would you mind doing something for me?"

"Not at all, Mose."

"Would you read me some from your Bible? I kind of like to hear written words speak."

"Sure, Mose."

Penny fetched her Bible and the three sat on a buffalo robe near the fire as she opened the book to read.

"I'll read some from Psalms, my favorite chapter."

"It don't matter as long as you read," Mose answered.

She read until the fire burned low and they put more logs on it for the night. They retired, each knowing the next day they would make Durango.

35

They slept late, arising about mid-morning, enjoying the warmth of the fire and eating more venison. After gathering their belongings, Blake Corley and Moses Baldwin carried them to the raft. Overhead the sky was gray and threatened more snow, but Blake welcomed the cloud cover for it would cut the sun's blinding glare. Moses tossed aside the tree limbs he had used to screen the raft from the opposite bank, then Blake handed him the near empty supply sacks, the buffalo robes, the blankets, and the tools.

Blake turned to start back to the cabin when he spotted a solitary man riding a mule down the Durango road. Blake ducked behind a tree and motioned to Moses, who dropped to his knees behind the sideboard of the raft.

"Can you make out who it is?" Blake asked.

"Not for certain."

"Think it's Donner's remaining gang member, maybe trailing behind Donner in hopes of catching us if we hid?"

"Could be. He is riding a mule."

The rider disappeared around a bend in the road.

Blake sighed in relief as he emerged from behind the tree. "Probably some dumb prospector from Kansas," Blake said as he started back to the cabin. "You coming? I want to soak up a little more warmth before I get in your raft again?"

Moses shook his head. "I need to do a little more with the raft." He picked up the tarp and unfolded it.

Blake trotted back to the cabin and knocked on the door to let Penny Heath know he was about to enter.

"Come in."

Entering, Blake saw her putting on her coat and covering her head with the shawl. She bent to pick up her valise, but Blake moved for it and took it from her grasp. They both looked around the cabin for anything they might have left. Everything had been loaded except the rifle and Blake grabbed it with his free hand and marched outside. "How are you feeling? Still weak?"

"A little, but the extra rest helped, that and the food. And having a bath and clean clothes makes a difference, too. I don't think I'll need to see the doctor in Durango after all."

Blake nodded. They walked side by side to the raft. They were almost upon it before Blake realized the change. Moses had tied the tarp around the sideboard, then draped the loose canvas top over the wooden compartment to block out the water spray. He was using a couple saplings he had cut to hold the flap up like an awning.

Blake tossed Moses a grin. "You're better at making do than any man I've ever known."

Moses's wide smile showed bright against his dark skin. "Didn't want Missy to get as wet as she did the other day."

"Thank you, Mose. The two of you have made me feel like a queen."

Blake stepped on the log and leaned toward Moses, handing him the valise and rifle. Blake jumped back on shore, then gave Penny a hand for balance as she eased down the log until Mose grabbed her shoulders and lifted her into the box.

"You sit down on the blankets I've stacked for you. The canvas top should keep you dry this time."

Blake started across the log, losing his balance for a moment and windmilling his arms before catching himself.

"Don't worry, Blake. It's just knee deep. You won't have to swim if you fall in." Moses laughed.

Blake grabbed the sideboard and climbed inside.

"You can sit under the canvas with Missy."

"Obliged, Mose, but don't you need help getting the raft back into the current."

Moses shook his head and grabbed the shovel as Blake took his place beside Penny. Moses used the shovel to push away from the rocks and gradually row the raft out into the current.

The current caught the raft and carried it sideways down the stream until Baldwin straightened it out with the rudder. The river was wider and the water smoother than it had been upstream.

When Penny leaned against Blake, he put his arm around her, pulling her tighter against him to keep her warm, he told himself.

"It's dry as a powder house under here, Mose," Blake called.

"I didn't do it for you, Blake. I wanted to keep Missy dry. You're just as ugly wet or dry."

"Thanks, Mose," Penny said.

Blake studied Penny and the odd expression on her face, hovering between a smile and a grimace. "What's the matter, Penny?"

"Just thinking."

"About what?"

"What I'll do once I get to Durango."

Blake didn't answer. He hadn't had much experience dealing with women, much less women he cared for. It didn't seem right to tell her how he felt about her. "I reckon I'll find work.

Maybe go back to Kansas and take up farming, though my heart's not in it." He wanted to say more, say how much he'd like for her to go with him wherever he went. But for all his good intentions, he did not picture her as a sodbuster's wife. She was meant for town where she could buy pretty dresses and go to church to read her Bible.

Penny sat silently for a minute, seeming as uncomfortable as he felt. "I guess I'll find work. Cook, take in laundry and ironing, do that sort of thing. If I can't do that, I don't know what I'll do. I just know the one thing I won't do again, ever."

Blake patted her on the shoulder. He wanted to say something, but he didn't know what to say that wouldn't sound foolish. He finally screwed up his courage to reveal his feelings, but before he could speak, Moses said something that sent his heart to racing.

"We've got trouble up ahead."

Blake poked his head out from under the canvas and looked down river, maybe a hundred yards away. There, standing on a huge boulder in the edge of the river was a man with a rifle across his arm. He was waving his hat and yelling something.

Blake reached for the rifle under the tarp and stood up ready to meet the threat.

36

Sheriff Stewart Johnson saw them out of the corner of his eye. Across the river and behind some rocks, he caught but a glimpse of them and might not have even seen that had not one of them jumped into the trees and another ducked behind what looked like a short wooden wall.

One man was white and the second was black. It had to be Blake Corley and Moses Baldwin.

Johnson was tempted to turn back and look to confirm what he had seen, but he didn't want to give away the fact he had spotted them. That fence he thought he glimpsed must have been the makeshift raft they had used to escape Alfred Donner and Luther Perry.

What he didn't understand was why they had stopped rather than floating on to Durango. He had smelled wood smoke in the air and seen a plume of smoke from a cabin, but he had figured that it was just another prospector sitting out the winter.

Johnson decided the two men were readying their raft for the float into Durango. Johnson knew they had the money, but what he didn't know was what they planned to do with it. Both men were failed prospectors, men who had toiled at hard, dirty work trying to get rich. Now, they sat on a fortune. Money had turned many a man's head and turned his step down the wrong path. Johnson knew it was his job to find out and find out quickly whether the stolen money had made dishonest men out of Corley and Baldwin.

Once the mule rounded the bend, Johnson kicked it into a trot, even though the faster pace sent pain jolting through the pellet wounds in his left leg. The throbbing pain had been manageable at a walk, but at the mule's jog each step seemed like a hot poker boring into his flesh. As he rode, he looked for a spot where he could command the river when the raft floated by. He would order them to beach the raft. If they obliged him, the money hadn't changed their honesty. If they ignored his command and, especially, if they fought him, he would know his answer. He would not only have to track down Alfred Donner and Luther Perry, but also Blake Corley and Moses Baldwin.

He knew he must find a place quick or the river would carry the raft beyond him and he would never catch up. About a mile from the bend, he spotted a huge flat boulder jutting out into the water. Despite the pain, he kicked the flank of his mule with his boot. The mule was game, plunging through the ice-crusted snow and using all his strength, but the mule had little endurance left. Nor did Johnson. So many miles without a saddle had left his tailbone virtually numb.

Glancing over his shoulder, he could just see the raft coming around the bend. He slapped the reins against the mule and it ran harder yet, finally reaching the boulder.

Rifle in hand, Johnson jumped off the mule, wincing at the pain as he hit the ground, his boots cracking the iced snow as he landed. He limped as fast as he could to the rock, clambered atop it and walked as close to the edge as he could, trying to disguise his limp. He cradled the rifle in the crook of his elbow, then took off his hat and waved it in a wide arc over his head. He yelled out their names and saw Baldwin look in his direction. Then he saw a second head appear from under a tarp cover. The head disappeared for a moment, then reappeared. Johnson saw Blake Corley with a rifle in his hand.

"Dammit," Johnson said to himself, "the money's turned them." He replaced his hat and cocked the rifle in his arm.

The raft came nearer and Johnson yelled out across the water. "This is Sheriff Johnson, land your raft so we can talk."

Both men leaned forward, like they couldn't hear his words.

Cupping his hands to his mouth, Johnson yelled, "Land your raft, this is Sheriff Johnson."

Then to Johnson's surprise, both men took off their hats and waved. Corley disappeared under the tarp a moment and returned without the rifle. Next, the prostitute stood up between the two men.

"Hallelujah, it's the law," shouted Baldwin, as he steered the raft closer to shore.

When the raft drew even with Johnson, Corley cupped his hands and shouted. "Our rudder's not too good. We'll drift into shore as soon as we can and meet you downstream."

Johnson nodded, releasing the hammer on his rifle and turning away from the river. He hobbled back down the rock and found his mule where he had left it, too tired to try to run away. Despite the throbbing pain, Johnson mounted and started along the road.

He figured the men could've been lying, but Moses's reaction was too genuine for it to be otherwise. He watched the raft shoot past, gradually drifting toward the shore and finally landing about a quarter of a mile ahead of him.

The three were waiting with smiles on their faces when he guided his mule down to the river's edge.

"We've room for one more," Blake said, "and this'll get us to Durango faster than your mule."

Johnson dismounted, wincing at the pain in his left leg. "I figure this is your mule, one you cut loose."

Baldwin eyed the mule and nodded. "Reckon you're right. You hurt, Sheriff?"

Grimacing, Johnson nodded. "I took a few pellets from a shotgun blast from Alf Donner." He eased to the water's edge and Baldwin climbed out of the raft to help him aboard.

"We saw him and another of his men pass late yesterday on the river road," Moses said. "We thought you might be the third."

"No. Donner killed Dick Pincham where you left the coffins."

"There weren't bodies in the coffins, but the money taken in the robbery," Blake said.

"I know about the bodies. I found them outside of town. Have you got the money?"

Blake nodded. "We were planning on turning it in in Durango."

"I know."

"Just how'd you know, sheriff," asked Moses, helping him onto the log and then into the raft.

"You'd never have stopped for me if you'd planned otherwise." He handed Blake his rifle, then took off his hat and nodded at Penny. "Howdy, ma'am." He grimaced.

"Let me look at your leg," she said without hesitation.

Blake helped the sheriff down and she jerked up his pants leg. His flesh was puckered and festering around several wounds.

"We need to get him to a doctor fast."

"Just a minute," cried Moses. "I want remove the harness from this mule, give it a chance to survive." Rather than unbuckle and unhook the leather lines and halter, Baldwin reached under the back of his coat and jerked his hunting knife, slicing quickly through the leather lines until all had fallen to the animal's feet. He slipped he knife back in the scabbard in the back of his britches, stepped to the raft and pushed it away from the bank, then climbed in. Blake held the shovel and pad-

dled away from land until Baldwin took the rudder and gradually guided the raft back into the current.

The sheriff exchanged information with the Blake, Moses,
and Penny about Donner's role in the robbery and in burning
down the freight building in Silverton. The trio explained how
they had managed to stay ahead of Donner, sawing the wagon
in half, then making the raft.

"Smart thinking, Corley," Johnson said.

Blake shrugged. "Mose is the one that figured it all out."

"It's called making do, Sheriff. I learned it in Alabama
back during the war."

Johnson nodded. "One thing, Baldwin, did you break
Buford's arm? He said you did."

"Sheriff," Penny broke in, "he was just . . ."

Johnson held up his arm and shook his head. "I was talking
to Baldwin. Did you break his arm or not?"

Baldwin swallowed hard, looked the sheriff in the eye,
then nodded. "Yes, sir, I sure did."

Johnson grinned. "Good for you. The bastard needed his
arm broken the way he's beaten the girls on occasion."

Shortly after dusk when the day teetered between light and dark, the raft rounded a bend in the river and the lights of Durango shone like a strand of jewels. The low clouds had begun to spit snow and the evening cold was setting in fast.

"We made it," Penny shouted, then hugged Blake and Moses, before stooping down and giving the sheriff a hug for good measure.

"We'll get you to a doctor as soon as we can, Sheriff," Blake said. "Moses tells me the freight office backs up to the river and it'll be easiest to stop there."

Johnson nodded. "That's a good idea. At least we can leave it under lock and key at the freight office."

Baldwin shoved the rudder and began to ease the raft toward the shore. He rode over a rock just below the surface, giving the raft a jolt.

A yelp slipped from Penny's throat, then a laugh.

"You may learn to swim yet, Blake. Just remember to shut your eyes and flap your arms."

"Tell you what, Mose, I'll take you up on a high cliff and show you how to fly, if you'll teach me how to swim."

Both men laughed, then Moses pointed toward the shore.

"I know the freight office's there, I just can't pick it out for certain. Sheriff, can you?"

Blake and Penny helped Johnson to his feet.

Johnson groaned at the movement, then braced himself against the sideboard. He pointed to a long, low building about fifty yards away. The near end of the building was well lit, but the back half was dark. "That's it. Looks like we're in luck and it isn't shut down for the evening yet."

Baldwin shoved the rudder hard and guided the raft toward the bank. Blake grabbed the shovel and used it to steer the craft toward land. They touched the bank just past the freight building.

Blake crawled out onto the log pontoon, picked up the chain and jumped for shore, using the chain to pull the raft into the bank. "Mose, you stand guard here. I'll get Penny and the sheriff up in the office and out of the cold, then come back and we'll carry the strongboxes in. Think we can carry two apiece."

"I can," Baldwin said, "but I'm not sure about you."

The sheriff shook his head. "How'd you two keep from killing each other on your escape from Silverton?"

"Penny kept us apart," Moses laughed.

Blake helped Penny to the shore, then stepped back to the raft where Moses assisted the sheriff until the lawman could reach Blake.

"I don't know if I can make it up the slope," Johnson said.

Blake slid the sheriff's arm over his shoulder.

Penny tugged her coat tighter, then moved opposite Blake so the sheriff could rest his other arm on her. Slowly the three of them climbed the slope and marched around to the front of the building, passing two horses hitched to a wagon. At the door Blake twisted the knob but it was locked. He knocked on the door frame, rattling the glass. The two horses stamped nervously.

Inside, a slender balding man with glasses and jittery eyes, looked up from behind the counter, bit his lip, and squinted toward the door.

Blake hit the door hard with his fist.

The clerk seemed paralyzed for a moment.

"Open up," Blake cried. "This is the law."

The man stood up, straightened his suspenders and stepped into the back room a moment, then returned, holding a key ring high in the air for Blake to see. He stepped around the counter and headed for the door.

"What do you need?"

"We need in, dammit. We've got some strongboxes that were robbed from the company on the Silverton run."

The clerk hesitated, Blake seeing a tremble in his wrist as he finally shoved the keys in the lock and opened the door.

Blake kicked the door open as soon as the lock clicked and barged in with the sheriff, almost knocking the clerk over. The office was hot with a nice fire in the stove.

"With all the robberies and things," the clerk explained, "I feared you might be planning to rob me."

"I'm Blake Corley and this is Penny Heath and Sheriff Stewart Johnson of Silverton."

"Me, I'm Ray Turpin, I just work here."

"The sheriff needs a doctor. Maybe we can borrow that wagon to take him."

Turpin looked over his shoulder and stamped his feet nervously. "I'm not sure if we can use that wagon, but we'll get him to a doctor when we're done, sure thing. We didn't know whether you'd stop here or not."

Blake moved toward a pair of chairs to deposit the sheriff. "I want to get the strongboxes up here as soon as I can. They've been nothing but trouble."

"There's a cot in the back where I sometimes sleep," Turpin offered. "Me and the lady can get the sheriff there, if you want to go get the money."

Blake nodded, holding up the sheriff's arm and allowing

Turpin to slide under it. Turpin sagged under the sheriff's weight and shuffled toward the back room, Penny helping as well.

Blake darted out the door and ran down the embankment to the raft. Moses had already unloaded the strongboxes and was waiting beside them.

"It took us a minute for the clerk to let us in," he explained as he grabbed two strongboxes by their handles and started back toward the building. He heard Moses pick up the other two strongboxes and follow him.

As he charged up the slope, Blake shook his head. Something seemed to be wrong. Something about the clerk's manner bothered him, something about what Turpin said didn't set right in his mind.

Moses caught up with him and walked side by side with him. "What's bothering you, Blake?"

"Something ain't right." They walked to the front of the building and stepped inside.

"Back here," Turpin called.

As he marched past the counter toward the darkened door, he remembered Turpin's words: We didn't know whether you'd stop here or not.

How could the clerk have known he was even headed toward Durango?

He stepped through the door into the dark, just as Turpin flared a match and touched it to a lamp.

There was only one way Turpin would have had any inkling they had the payrolls and that was if Donner had told him.

Blake lunged forward into the room, dropping the strongboxes on the floor and grabbing for his gun beneath his coat.

"What the hell's gotten into you, Blake?" Moses said as he stumbled over the strong boxes.

As the light took hold, Blake saw Sheriff Johnson sprawled on the floor. He spun to look at the other side of the room. His heart sank at what he saw.

Alf Donner held a shotgun on him and Moses. Luther Perry stood with one hand over Penny's mouth and the other holding a pistol to her head.

Donner grinned. "I wouldn't do anything except drop the gun, Corley."

Blake hesitated.

"Now, or the whore gets it."

Taking a deep breath, Blake bent and put the gun on the floor.

"Turpin," Donner ordered, "get the nigger's gun."

The nervous clerk did as he was told.

Moses growled. "You bastard."

Donner laughed. "Damn nice of you to bring the money to me. It'll be the last favor you ever do anyone this side of hell."

38

Alfred Donner waved the shotgun at Moses Baldwin. "Get over there by your friend and don't open your mouth or I'll kill you. You got that?"

Moses moved, but didn't say a thing.

Donner grinned. "If you three hadn't been honest, I'd been a poor man. But you just made me rich."

Luther Perry shook his head. "You mean us rich, don't you?"

"Why sure," Donner laughed. "We're all rich I meant. You don't know what we went through to get that money." Donner motioned to Penny. "Let the whore loose, Luther."

He obeyed and Penny scurried to Blake's side, sobbing. "I didn't know and I couldn't warn you."

Blake put his arm around her. "It's okay. Won't be any harm done when we get out of here."

Donner shook his head. "That's the shame of it, Corley, you won't be getting out of here alive. I even know where there are a couple coffins. You remember leaving them in the road for me, don't you?"

Saying nothing, Blake stroked Penny's hair, wishing he had said before the things he had wanted to.

"Luther, you and Ray start tying them up."

Luther grabbed a roll of cord and pulled his knife from his gun belt, then began to cut lengths of cord.

Blake remembered that Baldwin carried a knife in the back of his belt. He looked at Moses who nodded, as if they could read each other's minds. It would be foolish to go for the knife with Donner holding a shotgun on them, but at least it would give them a chance to free their bonds once they weren't so closely watched.

The sheriff groaned as Luther rolled him over and began to tie his hands behind his back.

"That'll be the last headache Stew'll ever have," Donner said.

Ray Turpin moved to Penny, pulling her from Blake's grasp. The clerk pulled her hands behind her back and tied them together as tight as he could, but Blake didn't figure that could be very tight as puny as Turpin seemed to be. He hoped Turpin tied him then he would stand an even better chance of getting loose.

"Sit the sheriff up back to back with the whore," Donner ordered Perry and Turpin, "then tie them together."

The two did as they were told and soon Johnson was tied to Penny. She could not hold his weight up and as Johnson's limp form leaned to one side, she fell to the floor with him, lying on her side.

Donner waved the shotgun at Blake and Baldwin. "Be real careful when you tie them up, they might try something. If they do, you better jump quick because this shotgun'll cover a lot of area."

Luther looked nervously at Donner. Then began to cut new lengths of cord with his knife. He tossed a strand to Turpin, then turned to Moses, shoving his hands behind his back and beginning to bind his wrists.

Blake hoped Perry didn't notice the tip of the scabbard hanging beneath Baldwin's coat. Perry, though, seemed more concerned by the shotgun Donner held. Blake felt a tremble in

Turpin's hands as he took hold of his wrists, pulled them behind his back and began to tie them together. Blake tightened his muscles and held his wrists slightly apart as Turpin bound them together. Turpin was too weak to pull his wrists together. Blake smiled. At least he would have a little room to maneuver his wrists and free them.

Then Perry shoved Moses and Blake to the floor and wrestled them to a sitting position, back to back. He wrapped the cord tightly around their chests. Blake took a deep breath and heard Baldwin do the same. They both knew that expanding their chests would give them a little more slack in the bindings. Perry made several passes with the rope until he and Turpin tied it off with a knot.

"Good, job, boys," Donner lowered the shotgun. "I guess all we've got to do now is load up the strongboxes. "Luther, why don't you do that."

Luther grabbed a strongbox, relieved to get away from the shotgun.

"Ray, you take their guns and put them out in the wagon, will you?"

Turpin nodded, picking up the three pistols belonging to Blake, Moses, and the sheriff. He ran out the door to the wagon and came back accompanied by Perry, who picked up another strongbox and carried it outside.

"Turpin," said Donner, "you armed?"

He nodded and pulled a small caliber pistol from his pocket.

Donner marched to him. "Let me take a look at that. It loaded?"

Turpin nodded again as he offered Donner the pistol.

Perry came back in for the third strongbox, grabbing it and scurrying out of the freight room.

The moment he did, Donner stuck the gun in Turpin's chest and pulled the trigger. The gun popped and Turpin fell dead, a puzzled look upon his face.

When Luther returned, he bent to pick up the last strongbox. "What happened to Turpin?" he asked, then realized the danger too late.

"He's not feeling well right now," Donner said, shoving the pistol in Luther's side and firing until the gun was empty. Luther collapsed atop Turpin. "Don't guess you boys are rich after all." He tossed the gun to the floor. "Nice thing about these peashooters is they don't make much noise."

Peashooter! That was it. Blake remembered the Derringer Penny carried in her coat pocket. If he could just get it, they would have a chance.

Donner kicked Luther's body, then moved to the strong-box, shoved the shotgun under his arm, and bent to carry the last of his fortune out to the wagon.

Instantly, Blake reached for the knife beneath Baldwin's coat.

Donner picked up the strongbox and headed out the door.

Blake wormed his arms beneath the coat and grabbed the hilt of the knife, but he did not have enough leverage to pull it from the scabbard.

"Get to your legs, Blake, break my arms if you have to but get the damn knife. Make do, dammit, make do."

Blake managed to get his feet beneath him and started to stand, He heard Moses gasp in pain as his arms were pulled up toward his shoulders. Taking a deep breath, Blake managed to jerk the knife free, but it slipped from his hands and clattered to the plank floor.

Blake slid back to the floor, his hands fumbling for the knife.

"Let me get it, Blake." Moses jerked Blake's arms around trying to find the knife.

"I got it," Moses said.

Blake heard Donner slam the outside door as he returned from the wagon. Then Blake felt the cold steel of the knife blade sawing at the cords binding his wrists. As the bindings fell free, Blake tried to hold them on so Donner wouldn't notice. He heard Moses set the knife back on the floor, then felt Baldwin rise up and push Blake about a foot. As Moses fell back to the floor, Blake realized he was trying to hide the knife by sitting on it. To his side, Blake heard Penny sobbing.

He looked out the door into the front room and saw the lights being blown out.

"Penny," he whispered, "you've got to do something, quick."

"What?" she sobbed.

"Sit up straight."

"He's too heavy?"

"It's our only chance. My hand is free if I can just get your Derringer."

Penny struggled, lifting unconscious Johnson part of the way, then falling back to the floor just as Donner walked in, holding a lamp in one hand and a tin of coal oil in the other. "You ain't going anywhere, whore."

"I want to die at Blake's side," she cried out.

"Damn touching. I guess that's the least I can do for you, seeing as how you made me a rich man." He put the lamp and tin of coal oil on the cold stove behind them, then grabbed the bindings that held the sheriff and Penny together. He jerked the two up and leaned her over on Blake's shoulder. Blake scooted toward her.

Donner stepped to the stove and took the coal oil tin. "It's cold outside and I just wouldn't want you to freeze." He began to splash coal oil about the room and then in the front room.

Blake shoved his hand toward Penny, searching desperately for her pocket. He found it and slid his hand inside, quickly wrapping his fingers around the small weapon. As he pulled his hand free, he hid the gun, then cocked it.

"Donner, there's something I need to tell you."

"I don't want to hear it."

"Yeah you do. We hid the money, there's only rocks in the strongboxes."

Donner tossed the coal oil can to the floor, grabbed the lamp, and came over to Blake. With his free hand, he grabbed Blake by the throat. "I already checked."

Screaming at the pain, Blake wriggled and managed to raise his hand to his side.

"What the . . ."

Blake pointed the gun at Donner's chest and fired both bullets. Donner's face went blank and he stood up, staggering backwards then dropping the lamp.

A wall of flame shot up around them.

39

Penny screamed at the fire and moved instinctively, but the weight of the sheriff dragged her to the floor again.

Blake felt Moses squirm to uncover the knife. Moses patted at the floor and picked up the knife.

"Take the knife," he yelled.

Blake shoved his hand behind him, cutting it on the blade before he was able to take the knife from Moses's hand. Blake wormed his wrist to his side and sawed at the cord around his chest.

The scorching heat seemed to seep through his every pore.

Penny screamed, then started sobbing and kicking madly at the encroaching flames.

Taking a deep breath, Blake pushed with all his might against the cord and it broke. He tumbled to the ground, grabbing Moses's arm, then slicing his wrists loose. Blake scurried to Penny, cutting the cord that bound her to the sheriff.

"Get Missy," Moses yelled. "I'll get the sheriff."

Blake shoved the knife in his belt. Scooping Penny up, he darted through the ravenous flames, past the counter, and toward the door. The heat was stifling and seared his lungs with every breath.

Blake heard Baldwin charging behind him. Seeing the door through the smoke and flame, he turned his shoulder and ran into it, knocking it open. He heard Moses's lumbering footsteps behind him. Quickly, they were outside, gasping for breath and yelling, "Fire, fire."

Almost instantly, the town seemed to converge on the building. Fire bells rang and people came with buckets of water. Moses put the sheriff in the back of the wagon, then helped Blake deposit the sobbing Penny there as well. Blake jumped in the back with them as Moses climbed on the wagon seat and drove the terrified horses down the street as Blake cut the bindings on the sheriff and Penny. As Blake watched, a crew of volunteer firemen dragged a hand pumper to the building and ran a hose to the river. They began to throw water on the fire.

Penny was sobbing and shivering, though Blake could not tell if it was from the cold or the close call.

"Stay here," he said. "I'll get the rifle and some blankets for you from the raft."

"No," she said, "don't leave me." She grabbed his arm and scrambled with him out of the wagon, then ran with him to the raft. The snow had covered the canvas and the flames reflecting in the water gave the makeshift raft an eerie look.

Blake pulled a couple blankets from inside and draped them over Penny's shoulders, then he got the rifle and Penny's valise.

She clung to his arm as if she never wanted to release him. He liked the feeling.

Together they moved back to the wagon. Moses stood up and motioned for them to hurry. They climbed into the seat and he rattled the reins.

"Where we going?" Blake wanted to know.

"Take Johnson to the doctor. The local sheriff gave me directions and told me not to leave there until he arrived."

Moses pulled up in front of a two-story building with the

upstairs windows lit. "Doctor, doctor, we've got a hurt man," he yelled.

Shortly, the front window lit up and a paunchy man with a gray mustache opened the door. "Bring him in."

"He was hit over the head a few minutes ago and shot in the leg a couple days ago."

Moses and Blake carried him in and placed him on a table where the doctor pointed. Quickly, the doctor examined Johnson. The doctor shook his head. "The leg'll take a while." He motioned for them to leave the room.

They retreated. Penny started to sit in a chair by the stairway, but paused at the sound of Moses's voice.

"I best wait outside and guard the strongboxes. I'm so sick of them, I'll be glad to get rid of them."

"I'll stick with you until we can turn them over to the sheriff," Blake said.

"Then I'm staying with the two of you."

They stepped outside in the snow and waited until the local sheriff arrived from the fire. He was lanky with the thick mustache and dark eyes.

"Why don't we go inside to talk?"

"No," said Moses, "we've got near a hundred thousand dollars in the wagon and we want to get rid of it. It was robbed on the Silverton road last week."

The sheriff nodded. "You stay here I'll be right back." He stepped in to see the doctor, then came back out after ten minutes. "Why didn't you tell me that was Sheriff Stewart Johnson in there?"

"We've got many things to tell," Blake said. "But would you take us to jail and lock up the strongboxes so we can be shed of them."

"Sure thing," he said. "Follow me."

They trailed the sheriff to the jail and helped him unload the strongboxes, placing them in a cell and locking it.

The sheriff spent an hour questioning them and then left

to send a telegram. It was another hour before he returned.

"I've gotten word to put you up in the hotel for the night and keep you in town. The president of the Animas Freight and Stage Line is riding the train in tomorrow to thank you."

40

After sleeping until almost noon in feather beds in their own rooms, Blake Corley, Moses Baldwin, and Penny Heath met in the dining room of the finest hotel in Durango. Moses and Blake ate ravenously, but Penny seemed troubled and ate delicately.

"Aren't you feeling well, Penny?" Blake wanted to know. She seemed cold to him and he could not figure out why.

Penny looked at him, gave a half-hearted shrug and toyed with food.

"You two want me to leave?" Moses asked.

Both shook their heads.

"What is it then, Penny? We made it to Durango and we got a night in a fancy hotel."

She sighed. "It's just that when we walk out of here, we won't have anything."

Moses slammed his fist against the table. "You'd have each other, if only one of you had the courage to tell the other."

Blake felt as surprised as Penny looked.

"It's true. You two've been pining for each other almost from the time I got in the wagon with you, but you damn sure haven't made do with each other."

Blake knew it was true and he could tell by Penny's eyes that she did, too. "At least we can have each other, if you'll take me?"

Though her nod answered his question, the tears in her eyes said more.

"And as long as you'll have me, knowing my past."

"You said you weren't looking back, but to the future. I left Kansas looking for riches. I didn't find gold, but I found you. That's plenty."

Tears streamed down her cheeks and she took his hand and squeezed it.

Moses cleared his throat. "Now that you've made do, can we order dessert so we can meet this fellow from the freight line and start looking for work."

Blake and Penny laughed.

At two o'clock, they were waiting in the hotel lobby when the president of the freight line arrived with the local sheriff.

He was a short, pompous little man with white hair and muttonchop sideburns. He wore white gloves, an expensive overcoat, and a tall stovepipe hat.

"Here they are," said the sheriff, introducing them to Collin Franklin.

Franklin shook their hands. "The company is indebted to you and as a token of our appreciation, we are issuing a five thousand dollar reward to be shared by you three and Sheriff Johnson."

Blake felt his jaw drop and he looked at Penny. Her eyes were overflowing with tears again.

"Thank you, sir," said Moses. "That'll help us make do until we can find work."

"Work, you say? I know of two openings in the company, managing the freight offices in Silverton and here in Durango? Your lack of experience would be more than offset by your honesty. Would you be interested?"

Blake nodded. "I'd consider the Durango job."

"I best pass up the offer, sir?"

"But why, Mose, you deserve it," Blake said.

Mose dropped his head. "Remember, I can't read."

"I'll teach you," Penny said.

"We won't open the office until the spring thaw. There's time for you to learn," Franklin offered, "if you want the Silverton office."

Moses nodded. "I'll take it if Missy'll teach me to read."

Penny nodded.

"And what about you, Mr. Corley? When can you start work?"

"Give me two weeks," he said. "I'm planning on getting married, married to a girl who'll read to me from her Bible every night."

Penny cried.